W9-AYS-453
SCARD

Note to Readers

In *Dream Seekers,* the Smythe family's American Adventure continues. John and Sarah have grown up and gotten married, but Father and Mother have had two more children: Phillip and Leah. The whole family is about to move from Plymouth to Boston.

While the Smythe family itself is fictional, *Dream Seekers* is filled with real incidents and real people. Roger Williams was an important person in the founding of our country. His teachings helped develop the idea of freedom of religion. And at the time of this story, Boston was building its first church. It's likely that boys of Phillip's age worked on that building.

As we see in this story, there were many peaceful Native American tribes who had good relationships with the English settlers. But there were also some tribes that fought against everyone.

We hope you enjoy Phillip and Leah's story of disappearing friends, mysterious Indians, and narrow escapes as much as we enjoyed creating it.

The American Adventure

DREAM SEEKERS

Roger Williams's Stand for Freedom

Loree Lough

CHELSEA HOUSE PUBLISHERS
Philadelphia

First published in hardback edition © 1999 by
Chelsea House Publishers, a division of Main
Line Book Co. Printed and bound in the United
States of America.

Library of Congress Cataloging-in-Publication Data

Lough, Loree.
Dream seekers / Loree Lough.
p. cm. — (The American adventure series)
Summary: When twelve-year-old Philip and his sister move with
their parents from Plymouth to Boston in 1634, they encounter
mysterious Indians and survive narrow escape.
ISBN 0-7910-5043-2 (hardcover)
1. Massachusetts—History—Colonial period, ca. 1600-1775-
-Juvenile fiction. 2. Indians of North America—Massachusetts-
-Juvenile fiction. [1. Massachusetts—History—Colonial period,
ca. 1600-1775—Fiction. 2. Indians of North America—Massachusetts-
-Fiction. 3. Moving, Household—Fiction. 4. Christian life-
-Fiction.] I. Title. II. Series.
PZ7.L924Dr 1998
[Fic]—dc21 98-19953
CIP
AC

Chapter One

The Hard Road from Plymouth

1634

As Phillip Smythe picked up a woolen sock he'd dropped by his cot, the whispering began.

"George says there's enough work to keep his family and *ours* fed and clothed for years to come! We'd be foolish not to—"

"But, William, we have no cart," Phillip's mother interrupted. "How will we get there?"

Phillip lay flat on the floor boards by the opening to the loft. He peeked down into the kitchen. Mother and Father stood near the hearth. Their heads were bent over a single sheet of paper. It was a letter from Cousin George in Boston.

"I'd never make such a decision without first praying," Father said. "I believe the Almighty wants us to join George and Katherine in the Massachusetts Bay Colony."

Mother turned away. Sighing, she covered her face with both hands. "I've come to love this place and these people so very much."

Not wanting to be caught listening to his parents' conversation, Phillip resisted the urge to punch the floor. *That's it, Mother! Tell him you'd rather stay. I don't want to leave Plymouth, either!*

"Abigail," Father said gently, his hands on her narrow shoulders. "You know this has always been a dream of mine. I want to be free and independent and able to provide all that my family deserves. As the Massachusetts Bay Colony continues to grow, more and more people are leaving Plymouth. There isn't much work for a carpenter here. Many of the people either don't want or can't afford the fine furniture I love to make."

He hesitated, then took a deep breath. "I believe it's God's will for us." He turned Mother to face him and lay a calloused palm on each of her cheeks. Looking deep into her green eyes, he smiled slightly. "Sweet woman that you are, you'll make dozens of friends. You'll see."

Tell him you won't see, Phillip silently urged his mother. *Tell him you won't leave all your friends. Tell him you've already left your home and relatives twice, and that you don't want to leave it all behind again!* Phillip bit his lower lip and clenched his fists.

Mother's voice brightened as she said, "I'll trust you to do what's best for us, just as you always have." Standing on tip-toe, she pressed her lips to Father's. "All that really matters is that we're together."

Maybe that's all that matters to you, Phillip thought, *but it isn't all that matters to me!*

He'd heard about the Indians that roamed the territory between Plymouth and Boston. Not so very long ago, the Pequots had murdered a fur trader simply for crossing their land! What could his father be thinking? Their family couldn't set out on another journey that would put Mother and little Leah in danger.

But wait. Perhaps it was nothing but a terrible dream. Perhaps Phillip would awaken and find that nothing had changed, that nothing *would* change in their lives.

But three days later, the conversation Phillip had overheard became all too real. At the end of supper, Father calmly announced, "We'll be leaving at first light."

Phillip placed his supper bowl on the table. He folded both arms over his chest. "I'm staying here. I'll live with John's family."

Father chuckled. "Whatever are you talking about, Phillip?"

Phillip had never defied his father. But he met Father's eyes and said, "I've known about the move for days. I heard you and Mother talking the day Cousin George's letter arrived." He sat up taller and lifted his chin. "I won't be going with you in the morning."

Leah, who had been listening quietly since their father's announcement, put down her bread. "If Phillip isn't going," she whispered, "then I'm not going, either."

"Now look what you've done," Mother scolded, patting Leah's dark hair. "You've upset her."

Phillip rolled his eyes. *Sisters,* he thought, *ought to be against the law. They are nothing but trouble and—*

"You are going with us."

There was no mistaking Father's tone. No mistaking the anger that darkened his brown eyes, either.

"But, Father, the rest of the boys—"

"The rest of the boys will do what *their* fathers think best," Father finished. "You're only twelve years old, Phillip, far from being a man. Until you are a man, you'll do as you're told."

The hard edge of his voice immediately softened as he got onto one knee and gathered Leah in a warm hug. "There, there," he crooned, "don't cry, my sweet girl. Phillip will come with us. Don't you worry." He punctuated his promise with a noisy kiss on her cheek, then released her. "Now, off to bed with the both of you," he said, standing. "We've got to get an early start tomorrow. It's a long ride to Boston, you know."

Phillip climbed woodenly up the ladder toward his cot. Slipping into his nightclothes, he said to himself, *They can make me go, but they can't make me like it!*

As always before bed, he fell to his knees and leaned both elbows on the mattress. Closing his eyes tight, Phillip leaned his chin on folded hands.

"Dear Lord," he whispered. "The Bible tells us we're to lay our troubles at Your feet. Well, moving to Boston is the biggest trouble I've ever known. Boston isn't home. *Plymouth* is! Give me a sign that You'll help me find a way to stay."

Climbing between the soft muslin sheet and the warm quilt his mother had made him, Phillip frowned and punched his pillow, hard. The action reminded him of Leah, who stamped her feet when she didn't get her way. *You're nearly a man,* he thought, *but you're acting like a spoiled little boy.* Perhaps this admission was the sign he'd asked the Lord to show him.

He rolled onto his side and snuggled deep beneath the covers. *I'll go,* he repeated mentally, *and I still won't like it. But they'll never know how I feel. I'll show Father that I know how to behave like a man!*

Chapter Two
Is There Danger in Boston?

"It's an arrowhead," Geoffrey whispered. The boy squinted harder at the stone he held in his hand. "And there's dried blood on the tip! I'll bet it belongs to a Pequot Indian. They're always squabbling over something."

Phillip leaned in to examine the sharpened stone and nodded. "Did you hear the story about the way they murdered that fur trader?" He gave an exaggerated shiver. "Skinned him alive, then hung him from—"

"*Hanged* him," Geoffrey corrected. "Mr. Williams says, 'Pictures are hung, people are hanged.' "

Phillip raised an eyebrow. He had no choice but to listen when his parents and teachers questioned his grammar, but he didn't have to endure criticism from a boy who was three months younger than he!

Bowing low at the waist, he put as much arrogance into his voice as he could muster. "Thank you *so* much for setting me straight, Geoffrey, m'boy. Whatever would I *do* without your constant care of my speech?"

Geoffrey frowned and shook his head. "You don't have to be so sarcastic. I didn't mean any offense."

The pout on Geoffrey's face told Phillip that he had hurt the boy's feelings. Perhaps Geoffrey wasn't as much fun as his Plymouth playmates, but he was the only friend Phillip had made since moving to Boston.

The only friend. Had it only been four weeks since the Smythes had arrived in town? On the day before they left Plymouth, Phillip's father had traded a highboy bureau for a rickety cart that seemed to have two square wheels. It creaked and squealed as it bounced down the highway, pitching and tossing its passengers—and the family's meager possessions as well.

Each time the load threatened to topple, Phillip was forced to scramble over the back seat to prevent disaster. After nearly a dozen trips into the wagon bed, he angrily climbed in with the household goods and stayed there. When he wasn't tightening ropes and adjusting stacks, he sat with both arms crossed over his chest, scowling.

He hadn't wanted to leave Plymouth in the first place. Was it his fault the family couldn't afford a better-built wagon? Was it his fault that his father had to drive the team the whole way so that his mother could comfort Leah? *Naturally* the chore of realigning their belongings fell to Phillip.

He'd been behind a chest when the cart finally stopped. A cheerful voice called out, "Hello! I'm Geoffrey C. Martin, and you must be our new neighbors. Can I help in any way?"

"Thank you for your kind offer," Phillip heard his father say. "I think we can manage."

Phillip had hidden behind a stack of straw-filled mattresses. He'd peeked around them to get his first eyeful of the chubby, freckle-faced redhead who had so proudly introduced himself as Geoffrey C. Martin. Phillip didn't have time for much of a look, because Geoffrey was off and running.

"Mr. Sprague! Mrs. Sprague!" Geoffrey shouted. "Your cousins are here, your cousins are here!" After the hugs and kisses of the Sprague welcome ended, Geoffrey joined in as the families unloaded the Smythe wagon.

Now four weeks later, guilt hammered Phillip's heart as he looked into his friend's brown eyes. So what if Geoffrey was smarter than he? What harm had come to him from being told that "pictures are hung" and "people are hanged"?

"Sorry, Geoff," he said. "Didn't mean to hurt your feelings."

Immediately, the pout was replaced by a bright smile. "Hurt my feelings! It'll take a lot more than a cross word from the likes of you, Phillip J. Smythe, to hurt my feelings!"

Geoffrey sure does like to use a person's full name as often as possible! Phillip told himself, grinning. He watched as the boy returned to his careful inspection of the arrowhead.

"A Pequot tool. I'm sure of it." He jammed the stone into Phillip's shirt pocket. "Maybe if we dig around a bit, we can find more arrowheads, or even the shaft to the arrow!"

Geoffrey wasn't John or Will or Samuel—the boys Phillip had known nearly all his life. He didn't like any of the things Phillip liked. He'd never climbed a tree, but he didn't seem to mind watching Phillip inch up a gnarled trunk. And though he said he didn't see the merits of sitting for hours on a rock with a fishing pole in his hands, Geoffrey had done it twice. "Just to keep you company," he'd told Phillip.

As he watched his new friend search for the rest of the Pequot weapon, Phillip realized that maybe he needed to make the best of his move to Boston. There wasn't much to like about this new town, but at least there was Geoffrey C. Martin.

When Phillip returned from his jaunt with Geoffrey, he found his little sister on his mother's lap. They were sitting in the rocking chair near the fire, bundled in a thick quilt.

"What's wrong with her *now*?" he asked, slamming the arrowhead onto the table.

"Shhh," Mother warned, a finger over her lips. "Leah needs her sleep. She has a fever."

"*Again?* I'd think she'd be sick of being sick by now. I think she's faking so she can get out of doing chores and—"

Mother pursed her lips and shook her head. "That'll be enough of that kind of talk, young man." She kissed Leah's forehead and wagged her forefinger at Phillip. "You know she's fragile."

He knew better than to argue the point. The frown above his mother's narrowed green eyes was a sure sign of being sent to bed with no supper. He'd be better off starting in on his afternoon chores. Anything was better than standing there watching his mother fawn as Leah faked another illness.

"I'm going to gather the kindling," he said, then softly closed the door.

As he headed for the woods behind the house, he kicked a stone. *It's not fair!* he told himself as he began picking up wood. *Everyone dotes on Leah every chance they get.* Back in Plymouth, his parents and siblings treated Leah as though she were made of glass. And when she came down with some illness—which was most of the time—it was only worse. At least John and Sarah had not yet made the move to Boston with their families. No doubt the minute they arrived, they'd fuss over Leah before even greeting Phillip. *Why couldn't I have been the baby of the family?* he wondered, kicking the stone deep into the brush.

"Hey, there, Phillip! Wait up!"

Phillip turned and waited for Geoffrey to catch up with him.

"My ma wants me to gather wood for the cook fire."

The boy amazed Phillip. Geoffrey hated gathering wood as much as he did, but he didn't seem upset by the chore. Did nothing make him angry? Did nothing put him in a foul mood?

"I'm fetching kindling, myself," Phillip said, adding a stick to his armload.

Geoffrey unsheathed his hatchet and began hacking at a fallen branch. "I thought you always did that in the morning."

"I do usually, but I would have gladly taken the soiled rushes off the floors barehanded, rather than stay inside another minute."

The red-haired boy wrinkled his nose. "Must be something terrible going on at your house to make you want to do *that* miserable job barehanded. Why, you have twice as many chickens in your kitchen as we have!"

Phillip put several twigs atop his pile. "It's Leah," he admitted, rolling his eyes. "She's got a fever."

"Has she always been sickly, or did the move to Boston do it?"

"I was too young to remember much about the day she was born, but I'm sure she was sick that day, too." Phillip hesitated, then shrugged. "After all, why would the day of her birth have been different from any other?"

Geoffrey straightened from his work. "At least you *have* a sister."

Phillip had overheard his mother and aunt discussing the

Martins. Geoffrey's parents had married late in life, and the boy would likely be the only child they'd have. "Do you see the way she fusses with his clothing?" Cousin Katherine had said, "and inspects him from head to toe. What *do* you suppose she's looking for?"

"I suppose you're right," Phillip agreed reluctantly.

"If I had a sister, I'd thank the Lord for her every morning and night. I think if she were as frail as Leah, I'd treat her like royalty."

Phillip's brows shot up with surprise. "Why?"

Geoffrey's usually happy face grew serious when he said, "Because you don't know how long she'll be with you."

When had they gone from talking about Geoffrey's imaginary sister to talking about his real one? Phillip wondered.

"Maybe if you were nicer to her, she'd be nicer to you," his friend suggested.

"Maybe. . ."

"Maybe if she were happy more of the time, she'd be healthier."

Phillip nodded. "Anything's possible, I suppose."

Geoffrey sheathed his hatchet and bent to pick up the branches he'd hacked from the fallen log. Stacking them in his arms, he added, "You'll never know unless you try."

Grinning, Phillip gave the boy a playful shove. "How'd you get so smart?"

"You have a lot of time to think when you're the only child," he replied, giving Phillip a playful shove in return.

Laughing, the boys headed home. Just before they reached the end of the trail to town, they stopped dead in their tracks. In the middle of the path stood the biggest, angriest looking Indian either boy had ever seen.

Chapter Three:
On the Trail of White Wolf

Phillip and Geoffrey looked from the Indian's honey-colored moccasins to his side-fringed trousers. He wore a breastplate of bone and leather, adorned with large white beads. An etched copper band encircled each huge bicep. Two stripes of red and a stripe of blue angled from his straight, thin mouth to his narrow, dark eyes. A leather braid that held four eagle feathers hung from his head. More feathers, shiny and black, hung from his belt. In one powerful hand he held a quiver, in the other, a bow and arrow. The arrow's tip was missing.

The boys exchanged worried glances. "Do you suppose the arrowhead we found this morning is his?" Phillip asked.

Geoffrey gulped and looked back at the angry warrior. "Could be. Do you think he speaks English?"

"Don't rightly know," Phillip whispered. "But I know this much: We'd better make tracks, and make 'em fast!"

Together, they began the countdown: "One, two. . ."

On the count of three, both boys sprinted forward. Geoffrey darted to the big Indian's left, Phillip to his right. The wood they were carrying flew in all directions as they ran full speed down the path that would lead them back to town.

"Pa!" Geoffrey hollered the moment they broke out of the woods. "Pa! Indians on the warpath! Hurry! Load the muskets! Indians on the warpath!"

Mr. Martin straightened, hammer poised in one hand, tongs still holding the glowing steel that lay on the anvil. "Whoa, there," he said, frowning with confusion. "What's all this about muskets and warpaths?"

Geoffrey stood panting, hands on his fat stomach, and between gasps told his father what he and Phillip had seen in the woods.

"Now hold on there just a minute." Mr. Martin set his work aside and rested a hand upon his son's shoulder. "I thought you went into the woods to gather wood for the fire."

"And I got it, too. Only I dropped it when we were escaping. He was tall as a tree, Pa. Tall as a tree and as big around as a barrel!"

The blacksmith looked at Phillip. "And were you gathering wood, too?"

"Yes, sir. Kindling for the cookstove."

"I suppose you lost your load escaping?"

Phillip nodded. "That's right, sir," he said, gasping for breath. "Lost it escaping—"

"From a Pequot warrior." Mr. Martin folded his arms over his chest and studied the boys closely. "Are you aware that the Pequots live far south of here?"

"That may be, sir," Phillip said, "but there's a Pequot here now—"

"And he's the meanest looking Pequot I've ever seen!" Geoffrey finished.

"How many have you seen?"

They exchanged a quick glance. "Well, I've seen Wampanoags," Phillip offered.

Mr. Martin smiled. "If you've never seen a Pequot before, how do you know this was a Pequot?"

"Pa, you should have seen him. He had war paint on his face and a breastplate made of bones—with animal skulls on it—and scalps hanging from his belt, too!"

Mr. Martin chuckled. "Scalps, you say!"

"It's true, Mr. Martin," Phillip insisted. He looked at his chubby friend. "He was big and heavy; he's sure to have left footprints on the path." He met Mr. Martin's eyes. "If you'll come with us, we can prove what we saw!"

Geoffrey's father stepped up to his furnace and tramped on

the bellows pedal to heat up the coals. Clamping the iron bar tight in his tongs, he shoved it into the glowing embers until its tip, too, glowed bright and hot.

"I have a lot of work to do here, boys," he said, bringing the hammer down hard on the curved end of the crowbar. "It's an entertaining story, I'll admit, but you should find someone who has the time to listen to it."

"But Pa, it *isn't* a story. We really—"

Mr. Martin brought the hammer down again, then submersed the tool in the water trough. The hiss and crackle drowned out his response, but his intent was clear. He did not believe they had seen *any* Indian in the woods, let alone a murderous Pequot.

The boys shuffled from the smithy's building, shoulders drooping and heads lowered.

"You boys gather that firewood right now, you hear?" Mr. Martin called after them.

Green eyes met brown as the silent warning passed between the two friends. Like it or not, they would have to return to the forest.

"I have my hatchet," Geoffrey said, patting the sheath at his side. "Why don't you borrow one of your pa's chisels? They're as sharp as any knife, and much more sturdy."

Phillip had been warned dozens of times about so much as *touching* his father's tools. Did he dare actually take one from the workshop?

"You can put it right back after we've gathered the wood,"

Geoffrey said. "Chances are, he'll never realize you took it in the first place, but even if he does, what would you prefer, to have your father tan your hide or have that Indian—"

"Wait here." Phillip ran toward his father's workshop. When he stepped inside, Cousin George was running the wide blade of a chisel across the turkey stone, while his father planed a trim piece made of maple.

Phillip counted himself lucky the Indian hadn't carried him and Geoffrey off and peeled them like hard-boiled eggs. If his luck held out, perhaps he could snatch one of the smaller carving utensils before either of the adults took note of his presence.

He grabbed the chisel nearest him, palmed it securely, then dashed from the shop. "Got one!" he announced when he met up with Geoffrey. "And it's sharp enough to carve the nose right from his face!"

Geoffrey wrinkled his own nose. "Well, let's hope we won't need to do any carving."

Weapons at the ready, the boys reentered the forest. They took slow, cautious steps and moved between the trees like stealthy wolves, remembering now and then to bend and retrieve a piece of their castoff kindling. Looking right, left, right again, they kept careful watch on both sides of the woodland path.

"Last time we met up with him, he had the element of surprise on his side," Phillip whispered, raising his chisel. "This time, if we see the Pequot before he sees us, we'll be safe."

Moments later, when they tip-toed to the forest's edge, carrying their firewood, Geoffrey let loose a loud sigh. "This is one cook fire I'm truly going to appreciate!" he announced, eyes wide as he grinned with relief. "Nobody believes what we say, and that means everybody's in danger. Meet me at our secret place after you've stowed your bundle of wood, and we'll plan how to protect Boston's citizens!" With that, he disappeared into his house.

Phillip and Geoffrey speculated on the appearance of the Pequot brave until the setting sun burned gold and red on the horizon: Was he a lone marauder, cast off by the rest of his tribe? Or was he a Pequot scout, sent ahead to mark Boston's citizens as easy targets for fighting men?

In a cave overlooking the Mystic River, Phillip and Geoffrey enjoyed privacy from the prying eyes of parents, village elders, and the boys and girls in Roger Williams's school.

Although no one from Boston had likely visited the place recently, the cave had welcomed pilgrims of the past. The proof was written all over the cold, damp stone walls. In faded tones of blue, red, yellow, and black, cave drawings showed people and animals during feast and famine and battle. When the Phillip and Geoffrey held their candles high to examine the crude drawings, the cave's dim interior took on an eery glow.

All was silent, save the occasional plop of water drops falling from the cave's ceiling and landing in an underground stream. The boys lay back, hands clasped beneath their heads, and studied the drawings.

"Do you think this is where the Pequot warrior lives?" Geoffrey wondered aloud.

Phillip shook his head. "I doubt it. There'd be some sign. Footprints, food, something."

Geoffrey nodded in agreement. "Where do you suppose he came from, and where did he go when we ran from the woods?"

Getting up on one elbow, Phillip sent his friend a nervous grin. "Maybe he *wasn't* alone," he whispered, hoping Geoffrey couldn't detect the fear that trembled in his voice. "Maybe there are *thousands* of Pequots roaming the woods. Maybe we're surrounded by savages!"

As if to punctuate his statement, a shower of powdery soil suddenly rained quietly down upon them. The boys sat up with a start and strained their ears, trying to identify the whisper-soft padding sounds that likely caused the dry sprinkling.

They were on their knees, ready to sprint from the cave, when Phillip said, "Footsteps!"

The sounds echoed in the hollow space, moving closer, closer.

Wide-eyed, the boys scrambled to their feet and sped from the cave, chancing a backward glance now and then. Not until they reached the edge of the forest did they speak.

"I forgot the hatchet in there," Geoffrey gasped, running a quavering hand through his red curls. "My pa will—"

"The chisel!" Phillip interrupted. "It's bad enough I took

it! When Father finds out I've lost it. . ."

The boys' gaze locked in an alarming note of understanding. They had two choices: Plead mercy to their fathers for carelessness and disobedience, or return to the cave. . .and plead to the Pequot for their very *lives.*

Chapter Four
The Secret Place

"Pay attention, boys," Mr. Williams scolded. "Where are your minds this morning?"

Phillip and Geoffrey didn't bother to look at each other. They had already discussed the necessity of keeping what they'd seen and heard to themselves. If Geoffrey's father hadn't believed they'd seen the Pequot warrior, how could they expect anyone to believe they'd nearly been attacked by one in the cave! Besides, telling what happened in the cave meant letting others know about it.

"Sorry, Mr. Williams," Phillip said.

"Sorry," Geoffrey echoed.

"Very well, then." The teacher continued his lesson. " 'God hath sifted a nation, that He might send choice grain into this wilderness.' Can anyone tell me what that means?"

When no one responded, Williams went on. "I believe it means that our purpose here in the New World is to build a city of God on earth. We cannot accomplish this goal if we continue to regard ourselves as members of the English Church."

The children looked at one another from across the aisle that separated the boys' side of the classroom from the girls', each hoping to find some understanding of what Williams had said in some other student's eyes. No one knew what their teacher was talking about, but Mr. Williams didn't seem bothered by their confusion.

"We must stop abusing the kindnesses of our Indian friends," he continued. "We came here uninvited, and took over their land as if it were our own."

He was pacing now. Back and forth, back and forth he tromped across the raised platform at the front of the classroom, hands clasped at the small of his back. "We must break with the Church of England, for it is no longer what the Almighty wishes it to be."

Some of the children had propped their heads on folded hands, trying to follow their teacher's words. Others fought to keep their eyes open, unable to concentrate on such strange ideas.

"If a man does wrong to his fellow man," Williams said, "then the state should punish him. If that same man holds uncommon religious beliefs or departs from the customary practice in a small matter like Sabbath-breaking, his offense is no matter of the state."

What is this man talking about? Phillip wondered. He'd heard his father and Cousin George discussing such things from time to time after Sunday services, and he supposed political beliefs had a place at the main family meal of the week. But what place did such talk have here in the schoolhouse? Phillip decided he would ask his father that very question after supper.

Leah had never attended school because Mother was afraid that she might get too tired and then get sick. As he walked home from school that day, Phillip decided that it was as good a day as any to put Geoffrey's good advice to the test. He would make amends with his sister.

The moment he entered the house, Phillip sat in the hard wooden chair beside the padded bench Father had made. "How are you feeling today?" he asked his younger sister.

She opened one blue eye and studied him for a moment. "Why do you ask?"

"Just wanted to know."

She levered herself up on one elbow and said, "My head hurts, I have a fever, and every bone in my body aches."

He looked at her face. *Really* looked at it. She was a pretty girl—if indeed sisters could be pretty—with smooth skin that reminded him of fresh milk, and lips the same shade as the roses that grew wild near the secret cave. She wore her dark brown hair in twin braids that fell over her narrow shoulders, and her large, long-lashed blue eyes were ringed with dark circles. Why hadn't he ever noticed before how tired she looked? Why hadn't he seen the weariness that dulled her eyes?

He laid his hand upon her forearm. Her skin felt dry and far warmer than his own. "Can I get you anything?"

Weakly, she fell back onto the pillow. "Some water would be nice."

Phillip hurried into the kitchen, dipped the ladle into the water basin, and emptied it into an earthenware mug. Leah drank slowly, as if even swallowing caused her pain. "Thank you," she said softly, handing the mug back to him. With a sideways glance, she grinned. "Did you overhear Mother and Father say that I'm dying?"

"Of course not!"

Her smile grew and she shrugged. "Well, you've never been this nice to me before."

The truth of her words stung like a hard slap. *Why* had he never been nice to her? Was it Leah's fault she'd been born weak and sickly? Just that morning, he'd stomped and pouted, demanding reasons for the unfairness of his own life. How fair was it that his little sister, who had never done a cruel thing in all her ten years, was forced to endure endless pain?

On his knees, Phillip tucked the thick feather quilt under her chin. "I'll tell you what," he said quietly, "as soon as you're well again, I'll take you to my secret place."

Her eyes brightened a bit at his promise. "Secret place? Where is it?"

He aimed a long forefinger in her direction. "Not a word to anyone about this, mind you."

Leah held up a hand as if taking an oath. "I promise."

"Not even Mother and Father?"

Smiling, she shook her head. "I won't tell a living, breathing soul."

Sitting back on his heels, Phillip grinned and wiggled his eyebrows mischievously. "It's a cave near Mystic River. There are drawings on the walls, very old drawings. Geoffrey believes they were put there by the ancients."

Licking her lips, she asked, "Drawings of what?"

"Deer, beaver, eagles. . . .There are men in robes, dancing around a fire, and women with babies on their backs." He leaned forward and whispered, "On a windy day, the drafts in the cave make our candle flames flicker, and the paintings look as though they're alive."

Leah's cheeks had pinked up in the short time he'd been with her, Phillip noticed. He handed her the mug again, waited for her to take a sip of the water, then returned it to the three-legged table beside the sofa. "It was Geoffrey's secret place first."

"And he shared it with you?" She sighed dreamily, then looked deep into her brother's eyes. "You're very lucky to have such a good friend." Her voice softened when she added, "I wish I had a friend like that."

What could Phillip say to comfort her? Leah had always been too frail to play outdoors like other children and too fragile to attend school or even Sunday services. What opportunity did she have to meet girls her own age?

Just then, an idea began bubbling in his mind. Phillip got to his feet and tiptoed from the parlor to the kitchen, certain that by the time he'd completed his lessons, the idea would be a fully formed plan. He'd make Leah's life a bit brighter, and he knew just the way to do it.

Phillip had almost forgotten about the hulking Indian he and Geoffrey had seen so long ago in the forest. As Phillip gathered the twigs and sticks that would start a blazing fire in the hearth, he smiled to himself. His plan to help Leah had worked out well. Very well. He'd never seen his sister happier. It was the first time he'd seen her cheeks glow rosy red from joy rather than fever.

Mary had always seemed to Phillip like a sweet and gentle girl—not that he paid attention to most girls. She was the perfect choice to be a friend for his little sister. He hadn't even finished explaining his plan when Mary had volunteered to visit Leah that very day after school. "I'll bring dolls and hair combs, and recite some poems she might like."

Thank the Lord I'll be out doing chores when she visits, he thought, picturing the pair of them oohing and aahing over rhyming words and dolls.

True to her word, Mary had stopped by every day for weeks. Every so often, she brought her friend Anna. The previous week, the three girls had baked shortbread cookies for a tea party. They'd made Leah a doll, and she hadn't put it down, not even for a minute, since Mary and Anna had given it to her. She had friends at last!

Phillip was clearing the supper dishes from the table when Mother said just that. "It's done wonders for Leah," she remarked, "having girls her own age to play with. It was a good thing you did, Phillip, introducing them to Leah."

Just then, Father entered the room. "Phillip," he asked, "what's this I hear about Roger Williams?"

"Roger Williams?"

"Amos Carter tells me he's teaching his strange brand of politics in the classroom. Is this true?"

"He talks about things like the separation of church and state," Phillip began, "and says that as Christians, we're neglecting our duties by not bringing the Word of God to the Indians—"

"Can you believe it!" Father said to Mother, throwing his hands into the air.

"May the Almighty forgive him," Mother answered, shaking her head.

Phillip didn't understand why Mr. Williams's teachings had upset his parents so and was about to ask when his father suddenly changed the subject.

"Did you hear? Little Mary Connor has been quarantined."

Mother paled. "Quarantined! But whatever for?"

"Measles. And she's not doing well, either, to hear Amos tell it."

Mother hid her face in her hands. "Mary was here, just day before yesterday. What if she gave her measles to Leah? Why, some say it can kill a healthy child."

Kill? Phillip thought. Surely Mother had heard wrong. Surely measles wasn't a *deadly* illness.

Father crossed the room in two long strides and gathered Mother in a comforting embrace. "Then we'll simply have to pray for all we're worth that our sweet Leah will be spared."

Phillip left the room, dragging his boot heels across the floor. *He* had brought Mary into the house. If a robust child like that was suffering because of the measles, imagine what the sickness could do to Leah. If she got sick, it would be all his fault.

How could a good deed go so wrong!

CHAPTER FIVE:
A Good Deed Gone Wrong

Boston was a beehive. If folks weren't buzzing about the measles epidemic, they were droning on about Roger Williams.

With the town clearly divided about his teachings, Williams had decided to move farther north. On his last day as their teacher, he had explained to his students that he hoped the people of Salem would value the wisdom of his words.

"The Massachusetts Charter is invalid. I hope to find Christians who aren't afraid to admit it," he bellowed. "If we're to establish a purified church, the government of this colony must be wholly in our hands!"

All the children knew was that they would miss their handsome teacher. Each child bid him goodbye, wished him peace in his new home, and promised to pray for him.

After the Sunday morning service that week, a small group of men gathered in front of the church. "Roger Williams may be a godly man," Pastor Jenkins said, "but he'd better learn to tame those independent opinions of his. Otherwise, the General Court is likely to vote that he be expelled from this country. They could force him to return to England!"

"But that would mean we've given in to the King," said Mr. Martin. "Besides, what he says makes a lot of sense. Public leaders shouldn't have power over matters of conscience!"

Pastor Jenkins' thick white brows knitted in the center of his wrinkled forehead. He aimed his index finger at the group in general. Then he focused on Geoffrey's father.

"Joseph Martin, my good man, that kind of talk is likely to get you in trouble."

Phillip and Geoffrey had been standing quietly to the side. *Why should any man's beliefs get him in trouble?* Phillip wondered. Perhaps it was a stupid question. But Mr. Williams had taught him that the only stupid question was the question that was never asked.

"I thought our purpose in coming to America was to gain religious freedom," Phillip said boldly.

Every head swivelled toward the boy. Children were to be seen and not heard. Still, Phillip's simple statement cut to the center of the discussion.

Pastor Jenkins smiled. "Why, of course that's *one* of the reasons we're here, son. But there must be a governing body to provide law and order. Without it, chaos will rule the land. Remember, with freedom comes responsibility!"

Phillip frowned. "But. . ."

Mr. Martin intervened, "Listen to what the boy says. Shouldn't there be a difference between the laws of the church and the laws of the state?"

Geoffrey's father met each man's eyes, then looked back at Pastor Jenkins. "If you pass laws that tell us what is a sin and what is not a sin, how can we exercise our free will, as the Lord intended?"

Jenkins bristled. He ran a finger under his starched white collar. "Well," he said, clearing his throat, "it's obvious that the church and the state must work together. Each must support the other, you see. The state supports the decisions of the church. The church proclaims the supremacy of the state."

"Then we haven't established a democracy, have we?" Mr. Martin said.

"What's that you say?" Pastor Jenkins asked. His voice rose, capturing the attention of everyone within earshot. "My dear Joseph, you're sounding just like that Roger Williams."

Leaning close to Phillip's face, he added, "And from the sounds of things, it isn't just the men whose minds have been filled with Williams's nonsense."

Just then, Father arrived. He clamped a powerful hand on Phillip's shoulder. "Your mother and sister are waiting dinner for us, son," he said. His smile tight, Father said to the group, "God bless your day, sirs!" Then he and Phillip walked briskly away.

As they headed for home, Father whispered harshly, "No son of mine will speak disrespectfully to his elders."

"But Father, I promise you. I didn't say one disrespectful thing. I simply asked one question and then Mr. Martin kept talking."

"They are the most important men in town. If I rile them— or if you do— they can put me out of business!"

Phillip glanced over his shoulder at the gentlemen on the church steps.

"I thought you left Holland to get away from that kind of power. Doesn't anyone care that Mr. Williams was run out of town just like you were run out of England? Why, a robber or a murderer would have received better treatment! He's a good man, Father. It isn't fair what the people of this town have done to him. He only wants what's right and—"

"You're very nearly a man, son. But when you behave like this, you show me you have a ways to go. One thing's sure. When you finally *do* become a man, you'll understand that things are rarely what they appear to be.

"Your Mr. Williams has some valid points," Father continued. "But his rabble-rousing is creating more problems than it's solving."

Father stood still and wrapped his big hand around Phillip's wrist. "I've said it before, but it bears repeating. *Until* you prove that you can handle the responsibilities of being a man, you'll do as you're told. You are *not* to spout another word of Roger Williams's teachings. Is that clear?"

"You won't hear another word from me on the subject," Phillip promised his father.

Releasing Phillip's wrist, Father's voice gentled. "It's just a matter of time before that man finds himself caught between a rock and a hard place. I don't want any of the Smythes—or the Martins, for that matter—to be with him when he's flattened."

The days slowly ticked by as the Smythe family waited to see whether Leah would get measles. She seemed no more tired than usual, so they tried to be hopeful.

There was one bright note. John and Sarah were due to arrive with their families from Plymouth any day. It would be so good to have them nearby again!

Though he had pretended to hate every minute of it, Phillip missed Sarah's good-natured teasing and John's playful rough-housing. Besides, it would be interesting to see how John and Sarah felt about the Roger Williams debate.

John, a carpenter like his father, would join the family

business in the center of town. Sarah's husband Jake, an apothecary, would open a shop near Dr. Turner's office.

Much as Phillip enjoyed fiddling with the tools of his father's trade, it was Jake's work that fascinated him. Learning to use herbs and other remedies to heal people seemed a wonderful way to make a living.

"It takes eight years of apprenticeship to become an apothecary," Jake had warned when Phillip first shared his dream with his brother-in-law. "You'll need to study hard and learn to read and write Latin."

That piece of advice changed Phillip's attitude about school. If studying hard would secure him a position like Jake's, Phillip was willing to work at his lessons far into the night. Now, he had more reason than ever to learn about remedies prescribed for the sick. Phillip had a dream. Someday, he would find a cure for Leah.

Meanwhile, there was the current threat of measles to worry about. Whenever he had the chance, Phillip followed Dr. Turner around town. He asked the doctor every question he could think of about measles. What are the symptoms? What can be done if the signs appear?

The proper name for the malady, the doctor explained, was *Rubeola.* This was a Latin word meaning *red* or *rosy.* According to the doctor, measles wasn't dangerous. "It's the other illnesses that often come with it that we worry about."

As often as possible, Phillip planted himself at Leah's side. He stared into her eyes, listened to her breathing, and inspected her skin.

"Phillip J. Smythe," she finally said one afternoon as she hid her face beneath the covers. "Having your toady face so near mine all day is sure to drive me mad!"

"You're beginning to sound like Geoffrey," he teased. "Calling people by their full names." He didn't mind her scolding. Not one bit. As long as Leah was strong enough to show anger, she was safe.

His pleasure died a quick death. Halfway through the second week of waiting, Phillip discovered that the whites of Leah's eyes had turned pink. A pale red rash flushed her cheeks and neck. Within days, she was coughing and burning up with fever.

"It's Rubeola, all right," Dr. Turner said after examining her. "Keep her warm and give her plenty to drink." The only other advice he could give them was to hope—and pray.

When he left the Smythe house, Dr. Turner tacked a notice to the front door. "QUARANTINE" said its bold black letters. Beneath the horrifying word hung a smaller warning: "No entrance or exit."

Because he was at work when the sign went up, Father would be barred from home until the illness was over. He would stay with Cousin George and his family.

But that was the least of Phillip's worries. His brother and sister were due to arrive. Sarah was expecting a baby, and John's wife had just given birth to their first son. They would have to wait until Leah was out of danger before the family could be reunited.

Phillip also worried about Geoffrey. Mrs. Martin had volunteered Geoffrey to gather wood and leave it on the Smythe's porch every morning. Geoffrey would be forced to go into the forest alone. Would he have to face the Pequot warrior?

Then there was the news about Leah's new friend Mary. The doctor had said that she had taken a turn for the worse. Her measles had worsened to quinsy. "Pray for her," he'd said. "If she survives the week, there may be hope."

Leah herself seemed to fade by the hour. And though the doctor had said the disease attacked only the young, Phillip was worried about Mother. The whites of her eyes had reddened. Soon she was coughing, too.

Chapter Six:

A Little Chicken Soup

As Phillip had feared, Mother had measles. With all the work that had to be done, he wished he'd been born with four hands rather than two. He ran from the cot in the parlor to help Leah, and then raced to the bed on the other side of the house to care for his mother.

By the third morning of the quarantine, Phillip had

established a routine. First, he'd fill the big copper kettle with water and set it over the fire. While he waited for it to boil, he washed beans and peeled and quartered turnips and onions. He then slid the vegetables from the carving board into the pot. Next he'd add the carcasses of the chickens his mother had roasted earlier that week. As he'd watched his mother do dozens of times, he added some herbs from the garden and stirred the mix well.

Though Leah and Mother insisted they were too tired to eat, he'd bring them each a slice of buttered bread. Standing with arms crossed over his chest, Phillip watched them until they'd downed every bite.

At least twice an hour, he changed the folded cloths on their foreheads for cool, damp ones. And as the clock struck every hour, he forced them to swallow some water.

At midday of the third day, Phillip spoon-fed Leah a bowl of soup, and then helped his mother eat hers.

"We're out of meat," she observed weakly. "You'll have to catch another chicken."

Phillip swallowed hard. Then he smiled brightly and said in a cheery voice, "I suppose I'd better get busy then, hadn't I? If I'm going to have it all cleaned and cooked by supper-time. . ."

Not until he stood in the small back yard did he allow his true feelings to show. Phillip grimaced as wondered which of the dozens of chickens he should run down. He took his time deciding, because the moment he chose one, the dirty work would begin.

Just take a deep breath and get to it, he scolded himself. Squaring his shoulders, he fixed his eyes on a fat red bird. He lifted his chin and prepared for the fight.

When Phillip grabbed for the bird, it scampered to safety. Every chicken in the yard protested with loud clucks and cackles. The flapping of their clipped wings and the scraping of their feet created billows of dust.

Choking, Phillip chased after them. He held his hands barely a foot off the ground, ready to grab when opportunity came.

Finally, he snagged his target. Tucking the bird under his arm, he headed for the stump in the corner of the yard. Many folks preferred to press the bird against a stump and then sever its head with a well-aimed axe. But Phillip's mother had always said, "It's far kinder to grab the chicken's head, give a good pull and a quick twist, and be done with it."

He could feel the hen trembling in the crook of his arm. Could he actually put an end to its life? It was one thing to unhook a fish that had been caught at the end of a long line or to aim his musket at a deer many yards away. In those cases, the hook or musket ball killed the creature. But in this case, he would kill an animal with his bare hands.

Phillip thought of his mother and his sister, lying pale and weak in the semi-darkened house. They needed nourishment, and plenty of it, if they were to get well. "If I must choose between their lives and yours," he told the quivering bird, "I think you know who the loser will be."

The hen tensed, then shivered even harder than before. "But don't you worry," he added gently, "I'll do it quick, like Mother does it. You won't suffer. I promise."

With that, Phillip squinted his eyes, clamped his teeth together, and did the deed. It amazed him how easy it had been to end a life. He sent a silent prayer heavenward. *Lord, let me never forget this feeling, lest I take a life You have created for granted.*

He'd seen Mrs. Martin pluck her chickens, feather by downy feather. It took hours of painstaking work to rid the birds of their fluffy down. Phillip decided he didn't have time for that. He would skin the hen, feathers and all, the way he and his father skinned deer, rabbit, and squirrel.

Once that task was done, Phillip stuffed the skin, with its feathers still attached, into the big iron pot in the hearth. Soon it was bubbling away. Later, he'd strain out the skin and feathers so that the fat from the bird could be used to make soap.

After taking care of the bird's skin, Phillip paid attention to the rest of the carcass. He threw out the chicken's vital organs, and put the meat and bones in the stew pot.

It hadn't been a pleasant task, but he'd done it. "A man must do what a man must do," Father often said. It made Phillip feel good to have done what was expected of him without complaining. His feet might not be large enough to fill Father's shoes, but Phillip believed he was well on his way to becoming a man his father would be proud of.

Pecking sounded on the window. Phillip sat up and rubbed his eyes. Had he dreamed the sound, or was there a bird on the sill, tapping to be invited inside?

"Phillip, say, Phillip! Are you in there?"

So, Geoffrey is the pesky bird! Phillip realized. He raised the sash and whispered, "What are you doing so near the house? You know we've been quarantined."

"I've been to the forest. There's a load of wood on your porch that's sure to last you 'til tomorrow, at least."

"Thanks, Geoff," Phillip said. Then, grinning, he added, "Killed me a chicken today. . .with my bare hands!"

Geoffrey wrinkled his nose. "Goodness gracious. Whatever for!"

"Why, I killed it for the stew pot, of course. Mother and Leah need to keep up their strength if they're to get better."

Sighing, Geoffrey admitted, "I know. I know." Grinning, he narrowed one eye. "Did the bird peck your hands? Did you get feathers up your nose?"

"If I was out there beside you," Phillip said, laughing softly, "I'd give you a good hard punch, right on the arm." But remembrance of how quickly the bird's life ceased to exist pinged in his memory. This was something important that he must always remember.

Standing on tiptoe, Geoffrey placed his hands on the high sill and rested his chin there. "So tell me, was it horrible?"

Phillip remembered the quiet *snap* that told him he'd broken the chicken's neck. "Yes, it was." Frowning, he added,

"But it had to be done, and so I did it. Now, can we please change the subject?"

Geoffrey's brown eyes widened in reaction to Phillip's sudden anger. "All right, we'll change the subject." The fiery brows wiggled mischievously when he said, "How's *this* for a subject: I saw him again."

"Saw who?"

"The Indian."

"You did not!"

Geoffrey grinned. "Oh, but I did. He was deep in the trees, just standing there, watching me gather wood." He looked left, then right, as if checking on their privacy. "Somehow, he didn't seem as scary this time."

"How's that possible?" Phillip interjected. "He didn't shrink, did he?"

Laughing, Geoffrey said, "No. He's still the biggest thing I've ever seen." His smile vanished and he grew thoughtful. "He didn't look angry. In fact, he simply seemed interested in what I was doing."

Phillip blew a stream of air through his lips. "Oh, as if he's never seen a boy gathering wood before." Rolling his eyes, he added, "The Pequots can't burn people at the stake unless they gather wood first!"

"I know it's hard to believe, Phillip, but I wasn't the least bit afraid of him. He looked. . ." Geoffrey paused, as if searching his mind for precisely the right word. "He looked friendly."

"Friendly, indeed. I think you tripped on a tree root on your way into the woods and thumped your noggin on a rock. I think—"

"Geoffrey? Geoffrey C. Martin, where are you?"

"Oh, no!" the boy said. "It's my mother! If she catches me over here, she'll tan my hide for sure!"

He was gone before Phillip could even say goodbye. Just as well, he supposed, closing the window. He should look in on his mother and sister, anyway.

As he waited for the tea water to boil, Phillip stood at the kitchen window and stared toward the forest, remembering Geoffrey's latest description of the Pequot. For a moment, he allowed himself to envy his friend's freedom to come and go as he pleased.

Phillip shook off the selfish thoughts. He would deliver cool compresses and warm tea and trays of nourishing food for as long as Mother and Leah needed him. And he'd do it in good spirits, too!

But the moment Leah and his mother were well again, he'd take off for the woods and hunt that Indian down. Then, face-to-face with the painted warrior, he'd see for himself just how brave a young man of twelve could be!

CHAPTER SEVEN

Nightmare in the Woods

Phillip trod softly, taking care to step on the hard-packed dirt of the path rather than upon crisp fallen leaves. The element of surprise had allowed the Indian to sneak up on him last time they met. This time, if Phillip had anything to say about it, the *Pequot* would know how it felt to be surprised!

The half-moon glowed bright white above the treetops. Its light slanted down through the leafy branches and rained upon the forest floor like silvery coins. Crickets and locusts sang their night songs, while tree frogs chirped. They seemed oblivious to the boy who moved in their midst.

Something buzzed by Phillip's ear. He lurched with fright, then smiled. It was only a beetle—not a Pequot arrow.

He had tucked his mother's biggest kitchen knife into his belt. Just for good measure, he carried a paring knife in his left hand. Phillip had a plan, and a good one at that. At first sight of the big warrior, he'd pull the big knife from his belt, and with a weapon in each hand, prepare to defend himself.

The Pequot might just skin him alive. But he would return to his village, Phillip imagined, and tell other warriors about the brave boy in the woods who fought like a man 'til he breathed his last. *His* scalp would be worn with pride on the Pequot's belt.

A twig snapped beyond the clearing. Phillip froze. Barely breathing, he craned his neck and strained his ears, squinting into the darkness for a glimpse of his enemy. Another crackle —this one to his left—caused Phillip to spin on his heels and face the direction from which he'd come.

The Pequot stood in front of him.

So much for the element of surprise, Phillip chided himself. He planted both feet shoulder width apart, hoping the action would still the trembling in his limbs.

It did not.

Four feathers had been lashed to the leather band around the Indian's head on their last encounter. This time, a fifth had been added to the beaded dark braid. Phillip had heard that eagle feathers were the reward for great acts of bravery. What deed had this man done to earn his latest prize? Had he beheaded a fur trader? Scalped a lone hunter? Skinned a boy alive?

The white stripes painted beneath the Pequot's brows beamed bright, making it seem that his eyes were as large and as cold as the moon itself. Beneath them, a streak of blood-red glowed menacingly. He'd drawn a false mouth around his lips, complete with pointed yellow fangs.

The huge man tipped back his head and cut loose with a war whoop. Phillip's blood froze. He couldn't keep himself from shaking. The Indian stared at him, long and hard. His murderous gaze said that only one of them would leave the forest alive.

Then the big man crouched, his feathered hatchet raised and ready for combat. As he came forward, moonlight glinted from the well-honed blade of his weapon. Phillip could only hope that, like the chicken he'd killed that morning, the Pequot would take him quickly and painlessly. He closed his eyes tight and began to recite the Twenty-third Psalm. *If you must die,* he told himself between verses, *die like a man.*

But wait. Were the moans he heard caused by the pain of the hatchet's chop or from the Indian celebrating his victory? Whatever its source, it was the most mournful sound Phillip had ever heard.

When he opened his eyes once more, he was flat on his back. *Amazing,* he said to himself. *The earth seems soft as a feather mattress.* Almost as amazing as the peaceful calm that had settled over him.

He blinked. Touching his brow, he searched for the wound that would eventually cause his death. *Odd,* he thought, looking at his fingertips, *not a trace of blood.* The Pequot's weapon had appeared keen-edged, but he couldn't have wounded Phillip without causing some blood loss.

Phillip glanced toward his feet and recognized the footboard his father had constructed from polished pine for his bed. The Indian must have brought him home. How else would Phillip have gotten into his own bed? *That* certainly didn't fit with the image of a brutal savage!

Was he dead or wasn't he? And if he wasn't, what was the cause of that dreadful groaning?

Phillip sat up and looked around. He crawled out of bed and crossed the room. Lighting the lantern on his mother's bureau, he peered into her mirror and studied his reflection.

Frowning, he realized the whole thing had been nothing but a dream—a very realistic dream—but a dream nonetheless. Feeling foolish, Phillip stifled a short laugh.

You're a brave man, all right, Phillip J. Smythe, he thought, replacing the mirror on the dresser, *to face a Pequot warrior in a dream and nearly die of fright!*

A quick check on Leah solved the riddle of the moan. A nightmare was causing her to toss and turn in her sleep. "Indian," she moaned when he changed the cloth on her forehead.

"Skinned him alive. . .hanged him. Burned him at the stake."

Phillip straightened her bedding, fluffed her pillow, and gave her a sip of water. Then he sat with her, stroking her hair until she fell asleep. After blowing out the lantern, he got back into bed.

Phillip clasped both hands behind his head and stared straight ahead. Shadows of tree limbs moved across the ceiling. He closed his eyes tightly and listened to the wind whistling outside his window. Branches scraped against the side of the house, sounding as though someone were trying to get into his room.

It seemed the Pequot's face was etched on the inside of his eyelids. Whenever he closed his eyes, Phillip saw the warrior as he'd seen him in the nightmare. He threw the covers over his head and recited the Psalm he'd repeated in his dream: "The Lord is my shepherd, I shall not want. He maketh me to lie down in green pastures; he leadeth me beside the still waters, he restoreth my soul. Yea, though I walk through the valley of the shadow of death. . ."

Suddenly, the words took on new meaning and importance.

"I will fear no evil, for thou art with me; thy rod and thy staff they comfort me."

Phillip repeated the Psalm five times before sleep gave him relief from his fears.

Phillip took extra pleasure in his duties the morning after the dream. Staying busy was a good way to keep his mind off the murderous Pequot.

He'd been house-bound with Mother and Leah for six days. Mother seemed to have whipped the worst of the disease. Color had returned to her cheeks. She wasn't having as many coughing fits and her fever was lower.

As she pinned her white bonnet to her head, she said, "Your father will be so proud of you!" Wearing a clean black dress and starched white apron, Mother hugged him fiercely. "You behaved like a well-schooled physician, Phillip. I'm sure your care was directly responsible for my quick recovery!"

Hearing her praises lifted his spirits, but then, Mother's compliments came often. His father's praise, however, came less often and had to be hard earned. If Mother's kind words made his heart soar this high, how would Father's praise make him feel?

When Geoffrey delivered the day's supply of wood, Phillip's mother opened the door a crack and asked him to fetch Dr. Turner. Several hours later, the barrel-chested man appeared on their doorstep. He placed his wide- brimmed hat on the seat of a chair and draped his long black coat over its back. Rolling up his shirt sleeves, he entered the parlor and knelt to give Leah a quick once-over.

He pressed his palm to her forehead and frowned. "Still feverish, I'm afraid." Facing Mother he asked, "Is she taking any fluids?"

Mother nodded. "Phillip has seen to it that she drinks a cup of tea morning, noon, and night. He brings her dippers of water all through the day, as well." She beamed at her son. "He also spoon-feeds her soup and stew."

She smiled at her son. "I don't suppose being cooped up with two sick women has been much fun, but you've made the best of it. I'm proud of you."

Phillip shrugged one shoulder and did his best to imitate his father's strong expression. "I did what had to be done, that's all."

"But you did it with a warm spirit," the doctor said. "It brought your mother 'round, quick as you please."

"But Leah isn't better," Phillip said.

Dr. Turner looked at the girl, who drowsed beneath the heavy quilt. "Ah, but she'd be much worse for the wear if you hadn't taken such good care of her. I'm sure of it."

Suddenly, the doctor squinted one blue eye at the boy. "But how are *you* feeling? Any headache? Joint pain?" He stood and placed a hand on Phillip's cheek. "Well, you don't seem feverish."

Smiling, he stood back and winked merrily. "I do believe the Lord has rewarded the care you gave your mother and sister by sparing you a case of the measles. And there's more good news for you, m'boy. Since you've been exposed twice over, it's not likely you'll ever come down with the disease!"

He ruffled Phillip's light brown hair. "Now *there's* something to thank God for!"

"How much longer 'til Leah's out of danger?" Phillip asked the doctor.

He put an arm around the boy and walked him into the next room. "I can tell you this," he said under his breath, "and trust you to keep it to yourself because you conducted yourself like a man this past week. We can't know one way or the other what will become of your little sister. If she's lucky, the sickness will leave her soon, as it did your mother. But complications could set in, like—"

"Like quinsy?"

"Exactly. Now, don't look so glum, boy! You did everything humanly possible for the girl."

"But I'm the one who brought Mary into the house in the first place. Leah was lonely, and I thought she could use some company. Mary's the one who—"

"Hush, now," the doctor ordered. He shook a finger under Phillip's nose. "There is absolutely no way to know how measles got into this house. Your mother might have brought it in after shopping in town. Or perhaps your father came home from the workshop with it. Why, anyone who crossed that threshold might have passed it on. So no more nonsense about it being your fault. Do you hear!"

Phillip nodded, more than a little relieved to know he hadn't caused Leah's illness. But the knowledge didn't help salve the news that his sister might not survive.

After refastening the buttons of his shirt sleeves, Dr. Turner shoved his hat onto his head and shrugged into his coat. "I'll be leaving now, Abigail," he said, smiling over Phillip's head. "Keep doing what you've been doing, and I'll stop by in a day or so to see how it goes."

Mother walked with him to the door.

"If she's no better when I see her next, we'll have to consider stronger therapy. Bloodletting, perhaps."

Mother nodded somberly. "Thank you for what you said to Phillip, Dr. Turner. He hasn't once complained, but I can tell he's been worried."

"He's a good boy," Dr. Turner said, squeezing her hand. "Very soon now, he'll be a good man."

If I live to be a man, Phillip thought, picturing the hulking Pequot in the woods. He was determined to find the Indian and see to it that no more harm came to Bostonians because of a brutal savage.

Somehow, Leah had heard about Pequot attacks on Narragansett Indians and white settlers alike. Hearing those terrifying tales had led to her nightmares.

He remembered his own nightmare, and the way the warrior had looked at him. Those dark, dangerous eyes sent the clear message that only one of them would leave the forest alive.

Phillip glanced over at Leah, sleeping peacefully. For now, at least, no savage tormented her mind. She was too small, too fragile and weak, Phillip decided, to have to dream about being bludgeoned by a beast wearing war paint!

His hands opened and closed at his sides, and his jaws tensed with anger as he admitted to himself that his and Leah's dreams had been a brutal reality for many settlers. What good would it do her to have survived this latest bout with illness only to face the savagery of the painted Pequot?

He might well die trying to stop the Indian, but the Indian *would* be stopped.

CHAPTER EIGHT
Midnight Escape to Salem

The quarantine sign came down the day before John and Sarah were expected to arrive in Boston with their spouses. Excitement over seeing them again, worry about Leah's health, and fear that the Pequot would return kept Phillip tossing and turning most of that long, hot night.

As soon as he was done with his chores the next morning, Phillip ran off to visit Geoffrey. He wanted to know if there had been any more sightings of the Indian.

"Geoffrey," he called when no one answered his knock. "Geoffrey, are you in there?"

A gate slammed. Phillip turned to see his cousin Thomas heading up the Martins' walk.

"They left in the middle of the night," Thomas hollered. "The baby's got colic, and I was up walking him so Mama could sleep. That's when I heard all the noise."

"Noise?" Phillip repeated, meeting him halfway down the flagstone path. "What noise?"

"Geoffrey whining that he didn't want to go to Salem. Mr. Martin hollering that he didn't remember *asking* Geoffrey what he wanted, and—"

"Salem!" Phillip's heart pounded as it had on the day his own father had announced their move to Boston. "Why Salem?"

"I wasn't eavesdropping, mind you. The windows were wide open because of the heat," Thomas said, his cheeks flushing slightly. "I was up anyway, because of the baby—"

"All right, so we've established that you're not a busybody," Phillip said, exasperation making his voice louder than he'd intended. "What else did you hear?"

Leaning forward, his blue eyes narrowing, Thomas whispered, "I heard Mr. Martin tell Mrs. Martin that he was sick and tired of Pastor Jenkins and his kind telling him what he was supposed to think and do and feel and believe. He said it was just a matter of time before he did something the town elders considered to be wrong. Then he'd wind up in jail."

Suddenly, Thomas struck a pose. He put his fists on his hips and set his feet shoulder-width apart. He furrowed his brow and tucked in his chin. Then he lowered his voice and looped his thumbs into his belt to complete his imitation of Geoffrey's father. " 'Might as well get while the gettin' is good,' I heard him tell Geoffrey. 'Before they make homesteadin' a criminal offense, too.' "

Deep in thought, Phillip didn't hear the rest of his cousin's mimicry. *So they've gone and joined Roger Williams after all.* Many times, he'd heard Mr. Martin and his own father discussing what Williams called "oppression of the state." Many folks were considering the move north because they feared the royal crown. Just last week, two families had packed up and left town. And now, Geoffrey.

Before you know it, Phillip decided, *all the good people of Boston will be forced to leave.* Phillip glowered as he stomped away, leaving Thomas alone in the Martins' yard.

"Say, I wasn't finished with my story," his cousin protested. The boy ran to catch up with Phillip. Falling into step beside him, Thomas posed a question. "Who do you suppose will move into their house?"

After a moment of silence, he added, "They must be desperate to sneak out of town like thieves in the night."

"They wouldn't have left that way unless they were afraid,"

Phillip pointed out. "Someday, the leaders of this town will have to answer to God for putting that fear into decent people like the Martins."

"But my father says the freemen are trustworthy. They are making prayerful decisions that are best for all—"

"Nonsense!" Phillip interrupted. "There was a reason Governor Winthrop resisted when the General Court demanded to see the Massachusetts Charter," he began. "He didn't want folks finding out they had no more control over their lives here than they had in England. Mr. Williams explained it all in class, remember?"

Thomas rolled his blue eyes and laughed. "You must be joking! I got some of my best sleep while he was spouting his teachings."

"Hundreds of people have died trying to reach freedom in this new world," Phillip reminded Thomas. "You've heard the stories. There were storms at sea, sickness, fights over the few personal possessions they were allowed to bring with them."

Phillip assumed his cousin's silence meant he was remembering how his own family had suffered to get to America. "Seems to me, we can't continue to run away like scared rabbits," Phillip said, plopping down on the ground. "My father told me he saw two men fight to the death over who was the rightful owner of a blanket. Isn't freedom more precious than bedclothes? And if it is, isn't it worth fighting for more than a blanket?"

Thomas stretched out on the ground beside him and leaned

back on his elbows. Faking an exaggerated yawn, he said, "For some reason, I'm suddenly very drowsy. You won't be insulted if I lie here and have a short nap, will you?"

"Sleep yourself right back to England, for all I care," Phillip snapped. "Maybe, while you're napping, you'll dream up a world where all men are free, because I happen to believe that if this government is allowed to continue silencing men like Roger Williams, the *only* place we'll be free is in our—"

"All right, all right," Thomas said, hands up in mock surrender. "But let's not forget who and what we are, Phillip. We're *boys.* No matter what we think or how we feel, we can't change what's going on."

"I say we *can* change things! If we're old enough to sign on as apprentices and old enough to pay taxes on our small pay, we're old enough—"

"Here's a Roger Williams quote that's sure to calm you," Thomas interrupted. " 'Let's not lose sight of the main subject, here.' The man was only a substitute teacher. He taught at our school for a few months. He never intended to stay on here—I've heard my father and yours say so. It's as the good pastor said. Williams stayed just long enough to stir up a vat of trouble."

"So what's your point?" Phillip asked.

"He was here, and he gave us something to think about. But now he's gone, and we have no teacher again."

Thomas took a deep breath and brightened. "Since it's obvious the pastor is sure to put an end to our good fortune all too soon, what do you say we enjoy our holiday from school for as long as it lasts and stop with the history lessons!" He dropped a hand on Phillip's shoulder. "Here's an idea: Let's go fishing!"

Phillip said nothing. Thomas, at eleven, was still very much a boy at heart. Didn't he understand what was going on, right under his very nose? Didn't he see how these events would effect his—and every Bostonian's—life?

Were you this immature and self-centered just one short year ago? he asked himself. He watched his cousin jump up, then half-run, half-walk, toward his house, first leaping up to rip a leaf from a low-hanging tree branch, then stooping low to inspect a caterpillar. When Thomas held the wormlike creature aloft and shouted, "Look! Bait!" Phillip could only shake his head and hope he'd *never* been *that* boyish.

Phillip hurried back home and arrived just in time to see John and Sarah and their families heading up the road from the opposite direction. He burst into the front door of their house.

"They're here! They're here!" Phillip yelled.

For once, Mother didn't tell him to lower his voice. She rushed to the door and threw herself into her older children's arms. Then she stood back to admire John and Hannah's baby.

"How's Father and Leah?" Sarah asked.

"See for yourself," Mother said. "But I should warn you that Leah is not doing well. We must not excite her too much."

After the families had quietly greeted Father and Leah, Jake cleared his throat. "Our patient needs some rest," he said. "And we have some unpacking to do. Maybe we should get settled and stop by tomorrow for another visit."

"An excellent idea," Mother said. She sighed. "It will be so good to have you all nearby again."

Phillip touched Mother on the arm. "The morning chores are all done and the stew is cooking over the fire. Could I go with John and Sarah and help their families get settled in their new homes?"

Mother's eyes twinkled. "And catch them up on all of Boston's news? Yes, Phillip, you may go. You've earned a change of pace after all your hard work. Just get back here before dark."

A broad grin covered Phillip's face as he hurried out toward the loaded carts. How different Boston would seem now that he could spend time with his older brother and sister again.

"And we'll attach leeches to the veins at her wrists, ankles, and neck," Dr. Turner was saying when Phillip returned home at sundown. "My assistant is out collecting a fresh supply as we speak. I'll stop by in a few days, and if she's still no better, we'll put them in place."

"How long will we leave them there?" Father asked.

"Oh, several days, at least. I'll be checking back now and again to see how she's doing, of course, but we won't see any positive changes right away."

"Thank you so much, Doctor," Mother said. "It was so kind of you to hurry right over."

"My pleasure," Dr. Turner said, jamming the hat onto his

head. "Now, if she worsens before I'm able to return with the leeches, you won't hesitate to summon me. . ."

Both parents nodded somberly as the doctor picked up his satchel and hurried down the street. Phillip glanced at Leah. She was deathly pale "She's not any better at all?" he asked his parents.

"I'm afraid not," Father said. "Dr. Turner says the quinsy has a tight grip on her."

Phillip frowned. Nothing, it seemed, made any sense these days. First Geoffrey's family had run away from their troubles like frightened children, and now a supposedly educated man intended to drain the very lifeblood from his sister. "Surely there's a better way than—"

Father lifted one brow. "There's no denying you did a fine job caring for your mother and sister during the quarantine," he said. "But nothing you did qualifies you to make medical decisions on Leah's behalf."

"But, Father," Phillip began, "look at her. She's so pale and weak. I'm afraid the leeches will suck the life right out of her. Why don't we talk to Jake? Maybe he has a better idea of—"

"Jake is only an apothecary, son. The doctor tells *him* what to do, not the other way around."

"Still, it seems—"

"Enough!" his father thundered. "You ought to be concentrating on things you *can* do something about. Returning my chisel, for example."

Phillip's cheeks reddened, and he hung his head in shame.

With all that had been going on, he hadn't had a chance to tell his father that he'd borrowed the chisel, and why. Or that he'd left it in the cave when the Pequot snuck up on him and Geoffrey.

"I want it back where it belongs by morning," Father said, accenting each word carefully. "Then we'll discuss what happens to boys who disobey and steal and lie."

Steal and lie! Why, he hadn't *stolen* the chisel, he'd merely borrowed it. And he hadn't *lied* about it, either. But his father's angry tone told Phillip it was pointless to explain now. He'd simply have to return to the cave and get the carving tool.

"By morning!" Father repeated. The sudden interruption caused Phillip to lurch with fright. "Yes, Father."

"You were awfully hard on the boy, William," he heard Mother say as he headed from the house.

"Life is hard, Abigail," Father responded. "But it'll go easier for him if I don't coddle him now."

Phillip paused outside the open window and heard Mother's deep sigh. "You're right, I know. It's just that it breaks my heart to see him so sad."

Father's voice softened. "He's not sad, my dearest Abigail. He's becoming a man. What you see is inner conflict. The boy he was and the man he'll become are at war for control of him."

Phillip heard his heartbeat pulsing in his ears. What would his father say next—that he doubted the man inside his son would win out over the boy? That he'd raised a sorry excuse for a Smythe?

"He's already fought a few of those inner battles and won," Father said. "It makes me proud to call him son."

The words caused Phillip to stand taller, throw back his shoulders, and square his chin. Now, more than ever, he wanted to behave like a man. . .like his father. He wanted to prove himself worthy of the man's respect, and he'd start this minute! He'd head straight to that cave and retrieve the chisel, even if it meant facing the painted warrior alone.

If the truth be told, Phillip wasn't nearly as afraid of the Pequot as he was of disappointing his father.

The half-moon glowed bright white above the treetops. Its light slanted down through leafy branches and rained on the forest floor like silvery coins. Crickets and locusts sang night songs. Tree frogs chirped. They seemed oblivious to the boy who moved in their midst.

The whale oil lantern lit the path. Phillip picked his way carefully through the forest, and the knife he'd borrowed from his mother's kitchen pressed reassuringly against his side. The similarities between what was happening now and what had happened in his dream were almost enough to get him running full speed back to town.

Almost, but not quite.

Phillip would not let his father down. He'd retrieve the chisel, and return his mother's knife as well!

Finally, he could see the cave up ahead. As the black sky loomed overhead and tiny critters scampered about nearby, the cave reminded him of a fable Geoffrey had told him. In the story, a giant troll sat openmouthed beneath a footbridge, hungrily waiting to eat anything that passed over its gaping jaws. Phillip forced himself to enter the yawning black entrance to the cave. In his mind, it looked too much like the evil troll's greedy jaws.

Finally, he was inside. Phillip held the lantern high, and felt strangely comforted by the crude wall drawings of the ancients. As his perspiring body adjusted to the cool interior of the cave, he looked about for the chisel. There, about ten yards to his left, sat the tool. A few well-placed steps deeper into the cavern and he'd have it in hand. Then. . .

Something went snap. Barely breathing, Phillip froze, craned his neck, and strained his ears. He squinted into the darkness.

Pop! That sound came just to his right. *I believe I'm dreaming again,* Phillip thought, teeth chattering with fear. *At least, I hope I'm dreaming.* Turning, he faced the direction from which he'd come.

There stood the painted Pequot.

Phillip sucked in a great gulp of air and swallowed it, as he had in the dream, hoping the action would still the trembling in his limbs.

It did no more good now than when he had lived this scene in his sleep.

Light from the lantern reflected off the well-honed blade of the Pequot's weapon. *Let it be quick and painless,* Phillip prayed silently, closing his eyes tight.

Mentally, he counted seconds as he waited to die. *One, two, three. . .*

At the count of ten, Phillip peeked through one eye. The big Indian was standing as his father might, feet planted shoulder-width apart and arms crossed over his broad chest.

Odd, Phillip thought. *He doesn't look at all fearsome.*

"Why does boy close eyes shut in darkness?"

Phillip could almost feel the ground tremble in response to the giant's deep voice. He licked his lips. "I. . .ah. . .I. . .um. . ."

"You do not speak the tongue of Englishman?"

Blinking in surprise, Phillip said, "Well, of course I speak English." Then, frowning, he added, "How do *you* know English?"

"Missionary," the Indian said, tilting his head to one side. "He teaches me to read and write name. Teaches of Jesus the Christ. Says Narragansetts no longer worship many gods."

"You're. . .you're a *Christian*!"

The big man smiled. "I listen to man in black robe." Shrugging, he added, "Not yet sure if what he says is truth."

Phillip pointed to the chisel. "My father sent me to get his tool."

The Indian nodded. "Ah, father is woodworker?"

Nodding, Phillip smiled. "Yes, he's a carpenter. He builds houses and furniture and. . ."

Frowning, the Indian said, "Important tool. Why do you leave it in cave, then?"

Phillip shrugged one shoulder and admitted, "Because

you frightened us."

Chuckling, the Indian placed his palm against his chest. "I?"

"We heard that all Pequot warriors are murderers," Phillip explained. "We thought you would—"

"I am not *Pequot*." The man grimaced, as though Phillip had insulted him. Shaking his head, he said, "I am Narragansett." With a sweep of his arm, the Indian indicated the land outside the cave. "More than enough earth for your people and mine to share. More than enough game."

"Well, I *thought* you were a Pequot, and I've heard stories about the things they—"

"Pequot not care if man is Narragansett, Niantec, white. They slay all. This is why White Wolf came to cave."

Phillip wanted to pinch himself. Surely he was dreaming! How else could he explain that he was standing in a cave, in the middle of the night, talking to a painted warrior named White Wolf?

"Why does boy show his teeth, like small dog?"

He hadn't even realized he was grinning. He'd never heard a smile described in quite that way before, either, and it made Phillip laugh. "I guess I'm just relieved to know you're not going to skin me alive and burn my bloody body at the stake."

Now it was the Indian's turn to laugh. He reached out and gave Phillip's bicep three quick but gentle squeezes. "Not enough meat to feed even Narragansett baby!"

Phillip drew back his arm, insulted. Why, he was the strongest, tallest boy in his age group. How dare this Indian say. . .

Did he say *meat*? So the Narragansetts *did* kill and eat white men! Phillip's smile vanished like smoke.

White Wolf chuckled. "Missionary calls this 'joke.' It should make you laugh, not make you look like you just woke a sleeping bear."

Joke! What kind of dream was this, where his tormenter told jokes and teased and. . .

Suddenly, Phillip admitted this was real life. . .as real as it gets. He didn't like the fact that the Indian had seen his fear twice in as many minutes. *Let's see how he likes to be reminded there are plenty of things to be afraid of.* "So, you're hiding from the Pequots?"

"Not hiding. I am here to pray." White Wolf held out his hands, palms up, then met Phillip's eyes. "You have seer in your village?"

"What's a 'seer'?"

"Seer speaks to gods and seeks answers to prayer." He thumped his broad chest. "White Wolf is seer."

"What are you praying for?"

"Protection. Guidance. Narragansett scout says Pequots plan to make war."

Phillip's eyes widened and his heart thundered.

War, *here* in Massachusetts?

Stories he'd heard about bloody Pequot raids raced through his mind, complete with pictures of slaughtered men, women, and children. This time, Phillip supposed, he must look to White Wolf as if he'd awakened *two* sleeping bears.

Chapter Nine
The Real Truth

Phillip had never felt more like a man. He'd walked miles in the dark, stepped bravely into a cave that might have been home to bears, snakes, or a Pequot, and had had a long, heart-to-heart conversation with a Narragansett seer. He smiled as he quietly slipped into the house. Stifling a yawn, he yearned for the soft mattress and pillows of his bed.

But first things first.

A moonbeam slanted through the open parlor window and lay soft across the rushes that coated the floor. Phillip followed the wide silvery path to where Leah lay sleeping in the parlor. He made a move to feel her forehead, then remembered his mother's practice of testing fever. "The hands can be warm or cool," his mother had said, "and cannot feel a fever like a mother's lips."

Phillip pressed his lips to his sister's forehead.

"What are you doing?" came the small voice.

Embarrassed at being caught in this tender and thoughtful moment, he stammered, "N. . .nothing."

"You kissed me."

"No, I didn't," he protested. "I was checking to see if you still have a fever."

"And do I?"

"Yes, I believe you do."

She smiled up at him fondly. "Well, whatever you call it, I think it was sweet."

Sweet, indeed, Phillip fumed. "What are you doing up at this hour?" he asked, hoping to change the subject.

She sighed weakly. "It's too hot to sleep. Where have you been all night?"

He slipped the chisel from his pocket. "Retrieving Father's tool, just as I promised."

Leah gasped and put a hand to her lips. "You went to the cave? Alone? In the dark?"

Grinning, Phillip nodded proudly. "Let me get you a drink of water, and I'll tell you all about it." He tiptoed into the kitchen, thinking as he filled the dipper with water that it *had* been a brave thing to venture into the cave after dark.

He tiptoed back to her bedside. Raising her head with one hand, he held the dipper to her lips with the other. "Just small sips now," he advised gently. When she'd had her fill, Phillip swallowed the last of the water.

"Did you see the Pequot warrior?"

"Well," he admitted, "at first I thought I had." Phillip smoothed the sweat-dampened hair back from her forehead. "Turns out he's not a Pequot at all. He's a Narragansett, and his name is White Wolf."

Her fever-bright eyes flashed. "You talked to a real live Indian? Oh, Phillip, you're the bravest boy I know!"

If you had seen me in that cave, he thought, *you wouldn't have thought me brave.*

"Tell me," she whispered, "what did he look like?"

Phillip sat cross-legged on the floor and used his hands to emphasize his words. "He's taller and broader than Father, with skin as brown as hickory nuts and eyes the color of mahogany. And he has long, shining black hair."

"And did he wear war paint, like the Pequots do?"

"His face was painted, all right, but he explained it was to make him more acceptable to the gods."

Leah frowned. "*Gods?* Whatever do you mean, Phillip? There's only one God, and you know it."

"Well, of course I know it. He knows it, too. A missionary told him all about Jesus. But he'd been a Narragansett long before Christians ever came to this land."

Phillip's voice softened with reverence when he added, "I think he's trying to decide what is the real truth—what his people have always believed, or what the missionary taught him."

"Why do they call him White Wolf?"

"Before he was born, his mother saw a white wolf in the forest. She believed it was a sign that she would give birth to a boy who would be an important leader of her people. So she named him for the strong and stealthy wolf."

"I wonder if my name comes with such a wonderful story."

Leah was struggling to take each ragged breath. Phillip took his sister's hand. "Just look at you. You're exhausted."

She closed her eyes. "It's this cough. It hurts to breathe. It hurts even when I try *not* to breathe."

Phillip's heart ached for her, but what could he do? He wasn't a doctor. Why, he hadn't even started his apprenticeship with Jake. Phillip got to his knees. "I'd better let you get some sleep."

"No. Don't leave just yet. Tell me more about White Wolf, please?"

Phillip sat back down, determined to stay with Leah until she fell asleep. "All right," he began, "I'll—"

"I'm so afraid, Phillip," she interrupted. "They thought I was asleep, but I heard them talking. If I'm not better in a few days, Dr. Turner is going to put leeches all over me." Leah's tremble began at her chin and went all the way to her toes. "I don't want leeches on me. They're slimy, ugly, *dirty* things, and—"

"Hush," he whispered, stroking her forehead. "You'll be

better long before they have a chance to put leeches on you."

Her long-lashed eyes fluttered open. "Oh, Phillip, do you think so? Do you really believe I'm going to be all right?"

No. I do not. At least, not in time to spare you the leeches. But I can hardly tell you that.

Phillip smiled brightly at his sister. "Of course you are. I'm praying for it night and day. And what does the Good Book say?"

"That if we have faith even as a mustard seed, our prayers will be answered?"

"That's right. Now, close your eyes while I tell you the story that White Wolf told me."

Phillip didn't care what *anyone* thought. First thing in the morning, he'd pay Sarah's husband a visit. Surely Jake would have *something* in his apothecary shop that would help Leah.

"Hand me the flour, son," Mother said, slipping on her oversleeves to protect her blouse.

When she'd been sick, Mother had promised to bake Phillip some corn bread. His mouth watered in anticipation of the treat. The water was boiling hard when she stirred in the coarse cornmeal.

Phillip had watched her make it often enough to know she'd stand by the simmering pot, stirring with her big wooden spoon until the meal absorbed all the water. When the mixture cooled, she would scrape it onto a floured board. Then she'd add cornmeal and work the dough until it could be shaped into tidy round cakes. By the time he returned, the treat would be ready to eat.

"I'm off to visit Sarah and Jake," he announced, heading for the door.

"Your chores are done, then?"

Phillip nodded. "The wood's been gathered and stacked, the bedrolls are stashed, and the snares are set."

"Say a prayer you'll snag a fat rabbit in one of them," she said, winking. He had just closed the door behind him when he heard her add, "And say hello to that daughter of mine when you see her!"

Sarah was in her kitchen when he arrived, fastening a snood over her long brown hair. He guessed she had just come in from outside, for the wooden platforms that kept her skirts out of the mud were still tied to her shoes. "What a lovely surprise," she said, hugging him, "to see you again so soon." She tweaked his cheek. "Folks are going to get the idea you miss your fat old sister!"

"You're not fat," he corrected. "You're with child. There's a world of difference, you know."

She lay a hand on her huge belly. "And I'm not old, either!" she pointed out. Then, sighing, she said, "I'm afraid I take up twice the space I took up this time last year!" Laughing, she added, "What brings you all the way to this end of town so early in the morning?"

"I came to see Jake and thought I'd say hello on my way."

Sarah planted a juicy kiss on his cheek. "So! You prefer his company to mine, do you?" Ruffling her younger brother's hair, she added, "Well, I promise not to let it hurt my feelings if you promise to tell me what's so fascinating about my handsome young husband."

Using the back of his hand, Phillip dried her damp kiss from his cheek. "He's not nearly as messy as you, for starters," he teased. Then, nodding toward the broom that leaned in the corner near the door, he added, "His work is more interesting than yours, too."

Quick as a wink, Sarah grabbed the broom handle and gently paddled his bottom with it. "How's *that* for interesting!"

Laughing, Phillip dashed around to the other side of the table. "Do you think you should be running back and forth in your condition?" he asked, dodging her attempts to smack him again.

She returned the broom to the corner and asked, "Tell me, Phillip, how's our dear Leah?"

The fun of the moment died at the mere mention of their ailing sister. "The same. That's why I need to see Jake. If she's no better in a day or two, Dr. Turner will start leeching her."

Sarah wrinkled her nose. "Oh, the poor little thing. Why, the very idea of having those horrible creatures on me would make my skin crawl!"

Phillip nodded in agreement. "We can thank God we've been so healthy and haven't ever needed such treatment."

Frowning, Sarah said, "Yes. We can." Then she sighed and

brightened slightly. "What is it you think Jake can do for her?"

"I'm not sure. A poultice, maybe. Or a tea of some kind. *Anything* would be better than draining the blood from her veins!"

Sarah slipped her arms into the sleeves of her apron, then tied it at her waist. "But Jake isn't in the shop, I'm afraid. He left early this morning to gather herbs and berries."

"Do you know which way he went?"

"North, I think. But I expect him home before dark. You're welcome to wait here with me."

"Don't have time," Phillip said, heading for the door. "Leah's getting weaker every minute. And if the doctor is allowed to stick leeches to her skin, I'm afraid that'll be the end of her."

"I'll say a prayer you'll find Jake, then, and that he'll know what to do."

Phillip nodded. "I'll pray, too," he said, closing the door behind him.

He walked and walked, for hours, it seemed, hands deep in his pockets. Phillip didn't know how it had happened, exactly, but when he looked up, he was surprised to find himself standing at the mouth of the cave.

A voice from within the darkness said, "Come, join me. It is cool inside."

"Good morning," Phillip said once his eyes adjusted to the cave's dim interior.

White Wolf nodded. "Sit," he said, "and tell me why your eyes are dull with worry."

"It's my sister," he began. "First she had the measles, and now it's quinsy that's plaguing her."

Compassion and understanding lined White Wolf's dark face. "Old men and children in Narragansett village also suffer from the spotted disease. Many died before the healer found the right medicine."

"Healer?"

White Wolf's jaw flexed. "How old is your sister?"

Phillip held up both hands, fingers spread wide.

"She has lived ten winters, then?"

"Yes. But she'll not live to see another, unless—"

"Narragansett people take care in passing knowledge of cures, for medicine cannot work without cooperation of all things in nature."

Phillip's brow furrowed. "I'm afraid I don't understand."

White Wolf drew his knees up to his chest and rested his arms there. His voice softened and deepened as he told this tale:

"Once, there was a small girl who rode through the forest with her old aunt. The aunt fell hard from her horse, and the girl could not wake her. Soon, night fell upon them. The girl became afraid of shadows and the sounds of darkness.

"Then she look closer at the forest around her. Seeing it meant her no harm, she had no more fear. The trees smiled upon her and spoke kindly to her, and promised no harm would befall her in their home. The girl slept peacefully beside her aunt.

"By morning, when their people had come to take them home, the old woman woke and named the girl Touching Leaves. From that day forward, Touching Leaves knew which roots and leaves and stems would heal her people."

White Wolf raised a finger. "It is rare for one to know the language of plants, to know how their gifts heal. Touching Leaves was chosen healer."

"Are you a healer?"

"No, I am seer. Black Eagle is village healer. He know many secrets."

"Like leeches?"

White Wolf winced at the suggestion. "It is a healer's duty to draw *poison* from the body, not drain *lifeblood*!"

"I promise to respect the secrets you share with me, White Wolf. Please, won't you help me save my sister?"

The Indian pursed his lips. "I will tell you what I know, but I must warn you that the white man does not trust Indian medicine. Some say it is evil. You could face their anger—or perhaps even danger—if you confess where you learned these secrets."

Phillip had heard terrible stories of men and women being burned at the stake. Would Boston's leaders arrest and jail him for the remainder of his life or burn him at the stake for using Indian medicines?

Leah's tired and timid voice echoed in his head. "I'm so afraid," she'd whimpered. No matter what it cost him, he would do whatever he must to save her.

He raised his right hand. "If I share the secrets," he said somberly, "I'll do it as you have, with careful thought. I promise."

Chapter Ten

In the Apothecary Shop

Phillip went home by way of the field north of town rather than through the forest, hoping he'd find Jake. He was about to give up when he spotted his brother-in-law dropping berries into a burlap sack slung over one shoulder.

"Jake!" Phillip called, waving as he ran toward the man.

"Well, to what do I owe the honor of this visit?"

"Leah."

Jake's eyes darkened as he grabbed Phillip's wrist. "Don't tell me she's—"

"No. No, of course not." He took a deep breath. "But if we don't do something soon. . ."

Jake shook his head, then returned to his berry picking.

"What's your opinion of leeching, Jake?" Phillip asked, plucking the dark purple blackberries from the thorny bush.

The young man's big hands froze above the leafy shrub. "I think it's a barbaric, old-fashioned practice that has caused needless deaths."

Phillip added his berries to those Jake had picked. "You don't know what a relief it is to hear you say that, Jake." Facing him, Phillip added, "What do you think of the Indians?"

Jake shrugged. "Pretty much what I think of white men, I guess. Some are murderers and thieves, and some are good, decent men. Why do you ask?"

"Because I met up with a Narragansett. White Wolf is his name. He's a seer, and he told me—"

"Whoa, there, Phillip. Slow down and help me make sense of your rambling."

"Well," Phillip began again, more slowly this time, "I'm sure you heard all about the Indian Geoffrey Martin and I met up with in the woods."

"Pequot warrior, as I hear tell."

He would ignore Jake's teasing grin. Once the whole story

was out, the man would have no choice but to help him. "We thought he was a Pequot at first, because, well, we'd never seen an Indian up close before. He had stripes all over his face and eagle feathers—"

"And scalps hanging from his belt. I know. I heard."

Phillip looked at Jake earnestly. "Turns out those were crow feathers. And what we thought were animal skulls were nothing but polished stones." He took a deep breath. "Geoff and I found a cave near Mystic River. We were in there talking one day, and a noise scared us. Geoff ran off and left Mr. Martin's hatchet, and I left Father's chisel. I went back to get it, and he was there."

"White Wolf?"

Phillip nodded. "We talked for hours. He's a good man."

"And he told you something that will help Leah?"

"He did. But I promised him I'd take care who I shared the secret cures with."

Jake chuckled as he plucked another berry from the bush. "There's no great secret to most herbal medicine."

"He thinks I could be in danger if I tell folks where I learned the secrets."

Jake wasn't smiling when he said, "Danger?"

"Because the townsfolk might think the medicines are evil. They might. . ." Phillip swallowed, picturing himself tied to a stake, with flames lapping at his ankles. "They might think I'm evil and. . ."

"Ah," Jake said. "I think I understand." He wiped his sticky fingers on his stained jacket, then extended his hand to Phillip. "You have my word. I'll be careful what I do with the information you're about to give me."

Phillip put his hand into Jake's and pumped the man's arm. "All right. It's a deal then."

Looking left, then right, he lowered his voice. "We'll need to work fast, because if we can't make the medicine and get it working in Leah soon, Dr. Turner is going to cover her with leeches."

Jake's brow furrowed. He put his hand on Phillip's shoulder. "Let's get busy then. Time's a-wasting."

In the back room of the apothecary shop, Phillip and Jake followed White Wolf's recipe for the medicine. Jake ground the dried herbs into a fine powder. The trick would be getting the brew into Leah without being detected.

Phillip came up with the idea of slipping the ingredients into a mug and passing it off as tea. For three days straight, he slipped the powdered herbs into boiled water. Then he sat at Leah's side as she drank it down. He watched and waited, hoping and praying to see some small sign of improvement.

On the morning of the fourth day, Phillip returned from emptying his rabbit traps to find Leah sitting on a tall stool at the kitchen table. She was bright eyed and pink cheeked.

"What are you doing up?"

"Eating soup," she said, grinning mischievously. "What does it look like I'm doing?"

Phillip met his mother's eyes and smiled. "She's eating soup? That's the first real food she's had in—"

"Nearly a month. Your father and I were afraid she'd wither away to nothing. Why, she's nothing but skin and bones."

Phillip's heart hammered with gratitude. Leah was going to be all right, and White Wolf's recipe was the reason!

"Your soup is much tastier than the brew Phillip has been feeding me the past few days, Mother." Leah crinkled her nose and puckered her lips. "It smelled even worse than it tasted."

"Why did you drink it, then?" he wanted to know.

"Because I knew you'd never do anything to hurt me." She smiled so wide that nearly every tooth in her head showed. "You're the best brother in the whole wide world, Phillip!"

"What's this I hear?" Father said, entering the room. "What have you been feeding her, Phillip?"

Shrugging, the boy grinned. "Just some tea, made with herbs that I—"

"I thought I made it perfectly clear that you were to leave the doctoring to those schooled to do it."

Phillip's smile vanished, along with his high-spirited mood. He'd expected his father would be grateful that the mixture had cured Leah.

"Show me this. . .this so-called *tea* you've been feeding your helpless little sister."

Leah's pink cheeks whitened and she stood on trembling legs. "Father," she said, her voice quavering as she held back her tears. "Please don't be angry with Phillip. Whatever he gave me made me better. I don't hurt any more and—"

"Leah," Father interrupted, speaking gently. "Go into the other room and lie down while I have a word with your brother."

She leaned against the table, blinking silently. "Mother? Aren't *you* pleased that I'm better at last?"

Mother gathered Leah in a hearty hug. "Of course I am, my sweet girl. Whatever would make you ask such a thing?"

Looking from Father to Mother, Leah said, "You're angry that Phillip gave me the tea. It's the very reason I'm better. That can only mean you don't want me to—"

"William," Mother interrupted, blinking back tears. "She's right. What difference does it make *what* helped Leah? She's better!"

"You don't know that yet. And neither do I." Father glared at Phillip. "You will tell me what was in the brew you fed your sister, and you will tell me where you learned to make it." He ran a hand through his hair, then shook his head. "What if we discover later on that there was a harmful ingredient in the tea? Have you considered that?"

White Wolf had told Phillip how the Narragansett healer had prescribed the tea for all who were sick with measles. The brew had brought most of them back to health. His Indian friend would not have given him a recipe that would hurt Leah.

Phillip chewed his lower lip for a moment, frowning. How would he explain to his father that he couldn't talk about the recipe—or where he'd gotten it—without exposing White Wolf? He'd given his word to the Indian. Hadn't his father taught him that a man's word was his bond?

Which was worse? To disobey his father's rule that a man must be true to his word? Or to disobey his father's command to share White Wolf's healing remedy?

"I'm sorry, Father, but I can't tell you what you want to know."

The next days passed in uncomfortable silence. Father spent as much time at the woodworking shop as possible and made no secret of the fact that he was avoiding his youngest son.

Phillip didn't sleep well, and he lost his appetite. Though he searched time and again for a way to please his father without betraying his promise, he couldn't come up with a solution.

He spent more and more time at Sarah's or at John's. One afternoon, he was sitting on a bench outside his brother's back door, when John sat down beside him.

"You look as though you bear the weight of the world on your shoulders," he said, slipping an arm around the boy's shoulders. "Do you want to tell me what has you looking so glum?"

"How much time do you have?" Phillip answered, a wry grin on his tired face.

John shook his head. "It's not an easy thing you're doing, going against Father. I don't envy you one bit."

"To envy me now, you'd have to be the world's biggest

fool. Besides, I'm not going against him. I'm doing exactly what he told me to do."

Phillip explained that he'd given his word to a friend. To tell Father what he wanted to know would break his promise.

"Still. . .don't you think it would be easier to tell Father what he wants to know?"

Phillip shrugged, leaned forward, and balanced his elbows on his knees.

"It's just this plain. I won't let them take Leah's blood. Even if she wasn't terrified at the prospect of having leeches stuck to her—and she cried herself to sleep worrying about it, I'll have you know—it's ridiculous to assume that taking blood can cure anything."

Phillip met his brother's eyes. "Tell me, John, what would you have done in my place?"

John stood up and pocketed both his hands. "I honestly don't know. I hope I'd have the strength of character to do what you're doing, Phillip."

Phillip stood, too. As he headed toward home, he decided to count his blessings. John had all but said he admired his younger brother. Leah would survive. He had a trusted friend in White Wolf. Only one thing could have made Phillip happier: To have Father's respect.

Chapter Eleven
The Accident

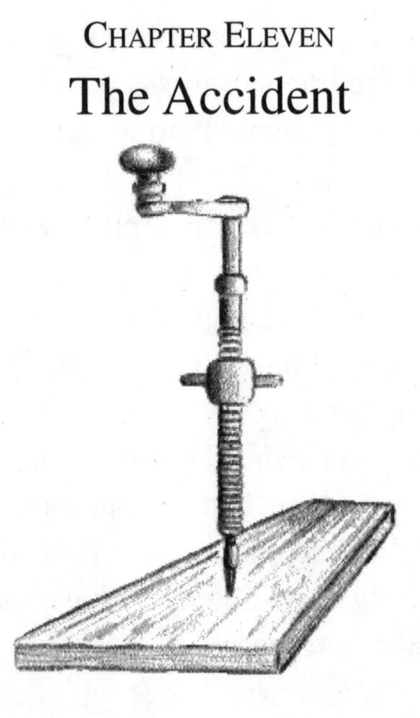

"Send up the hammer," Father called down to his cousin.

George set his brace and bit aside and rummaged through the big leather-handled tool box that contained levels, squares, a chalk box, and several gauges and pincers. They had been fastening roof rafters to joists, so George was fairly sure he would need the claw-edged mallet rather than the long-handled martel. He got the tool and laid it in the bottom of a wooden bucket. "There she is," he hollered, tugging the rope knotted around its handle. "Pull 'er up!"

Father squatted to reach for the other end of the rope, which he'd tied to the ladder's top rung.

"Watch your step, man!" George warned. "You're trompin' on loose boards, and—"

A scaffolding board tilted beneath Father's feet. The moment seemed to hang in time as he teetered helplessly at the edge of the feed store roof.

Phillip, who'd been next door baling hay for the new smithy, couldn't believe his eyes. He raced forward, wondering if he'd make it in time to put his idea into action.

Father's arms windmilled. His legs pedaled in an attempt to regain his balance. It was no use. He plummeted toward the hard-packed ground like a giant cannonball.

Phillip put everything he had into his dash, bending as he went to grab a corner of the stable boy's mattress. Would he be quick enough to place it beneath his father? And if he was, would the pad be thick enough to soften his landing?

Phillip believed he'd hear that dreadful *thud* for the rest of his life.

Father lay silent and still as a corpse. Phillip dropped to his knees and took Father's hand. It was not a good sign, he knew, that a small trickle of blood oozed from the corner of the man's mouth. Thankfully, he was breathing.

"Father," Phillip said, patting his hand. "Father?"

Father grimaced and groaned. "I can't move, son," he gasped. "Can't move. . .and can't see." Then he passed out. Father was carried home, but he never opened his eyes again. Phillip rushed to get Dr. Turner, but he wasn't at all surprised that the doctor had no cure.

"He's broken his left leg and his right arm," the man told Mother. "I'm fairly certain he's cracked a few ribs as well."

Mother had always been surprisingly strong for someone as tiny as she was. So it surprised Phillip when her pink-cheeked face went white and she slumped into a chair.

"Will. . .will he live?" she asked from behind her hands.

Dr. Turner placed a hand on her shoulder and gave a slight squeeze. "It's far too soon to say, I'm afraid. For now, there's nothing we can do but wait. . .and pray."

Phillip turned toward the window to hide his anger. He gripped the sill so tightly that his knuckles ached. *Wait and pray,* he repeated. *Is that the only thing the man learned in medical school?* Dr. Turner had graduated from Pembroke, the same college Roger Williams had attended. Had they taught him *nothing*?

"Phillip," the doctor was saying now, "your mother needs you. Pull yourself together, for her sake and your father's."

He spun around and met the physician's eyes. "Naturally, I'll do whatever is required of me," he spat, furious that the man would assume otherwise.

How dare he dole out advice at a time like this? How dare he stand there making only the most obvious statements! Why *didn't* the doctor have an answer for Mother? Why didn't he know what was wrong with Father? Where was the medicine that would end his father's pain? And where was the cure to bring him back to consciousness?

"When your mother is more up to it, I want you to tell her that I'll forego my bill for this visit. Your father will be laid up quite awhile," the doctor said, more to himself than to Phillip.

"Bill?" the boy repeated, a sarcastic laugh punctuating his question. "*Bill,* he says! Whatever would you charge us for, doctor? The amazing advice that Pastor Jenkins would gladly give for free?" He tucked in his chin and did his best to mimic the doctor's voice. " 'There's nothing we can do but wait and pray.' "

Dr. Turner's leathery face turned beet red. "I understand that you're upset, son, so I'll overlook your mockery and disrespect."

Phillip narrowed his eyes and leaned forward. "Thank you so kindly for your compassion and understanding, sir," he said between clenched teeth. "Now, if you'll forgive me, I have my father's work to do."

The doctor's cheeks puffed in and out as he struggled for self-control. Finally he whipped his wide-brimmed hat from the wall peg beside the door and turned to face Phillip.

With one hand on the door knob, he ground out, "Do

yourself a favor, *boy*. Spend a few minutes with the Good Book." He shoved the hat onto his balding head. "You could do with a long lesson on respecting your elders." With that, he grabbed his bag and stormed from the house.

He was halfway down the walk when Phillip slammed the door. "I'll respect those that deserve it," he muttered.

When he turned around, Mother stood before him. Her eyes swam with tears. "You've given me reason to feel many emotions, son—love, joy, pride. But until this moment, I've never had cause to be ashamed of you. Have you lost your senses, talking to Dr. Turner that way?"

Phillip's heart sank. He'd shouldered the responsibility of balancing his studies with his chores. He'd beat down his childish jealousy of Leah and had made a friend of her as a result. He'd faced his fears head-on by returning to the cave alone. And he had endured his father's anger at keeping White Wolf's recipe a secret and kept his word to the Indian as well. Phillip could stand just about anything, he believed, except the sad-eyed disapproval of his mother.

"You owe him an apology," she said matter-of-factly. Lifting her chin, she dried her eyes with a corner of her apron. Then she turned her back on him. Sitting on the edge of the bed, she took her husband's hand in hers. "Cousin George will tell you what must be done."

Just like that, she'd dismissed him. Phillip took one last look at his father lying motionless and pale on the cot against the wall. He'd never seen his father helpless, and Phillip didn't know what to make of it.

The plan was simple: Step straight into Father's duties and work at least as hard as he would have. Phillip would show them. He'd show them all that he was more than a boy with silly notions. He was a young man whose opinions deserved respect!

His plan died a quick death.

He wasn't even halfway up the ladder before his cousin grabbed his ankle.

"You'll climb right down from there, boy," he demanded, "and keep both of your boots flat on the ground."

"But Cousin George," Phillip protested, "I'm here to work in Father's stead. I *will* do his work. I promise. And I *will* do it well."

"You will *do,*" Cousin George replied, "as you're told."

George dropped a hand on Phillip's shoulder. "I don't mean to bark at you, son. It's just that sometimes things pile up, and we don't behave as we ought."

He sighed. "That accident was no one's fault—least of all, yours. Why, if you hadn't had the foresight to slide that mattress under him, your father would likely be six feet under right now."

Phillip winced, but George didn't appear to have noticed. "I'll do the roofing work because I'm better trained at it," he said, fastening his leather apron around his ample waist. "If you're of a mind to learn it, I'll teach you, in good time."

He tucked a handful of long, square-headed nails into one pocket and dropped a well-worn hammer into the other. " 'Til you *are* of a mind to learn, you'll stay where you're safe."

George lifted one brow. "We don't need another out-of-work Smythe on our hands, now do we?" Winking, he quickly added, "And there's no need to fret about whether or not you'll pull your share of the load."

He nodded toward the stack of lumber behind Phillip. "There's more than enough to do down here on solid ground to keep you busy from dawn to dusk!" With a hearty laugh and a hard slap to the boy's back, George headed up the ladder.

They toiled nonstop until the red sun had set. His father's cousin, Phillip soon discovered, believed the day went faster if a man worked with a song in his heart. Phillip didn't realize so many songs had been written, let alone that any one person could know them all. George whistled and hummed and sang the whole day long, and Phillip thanked God for the pleasant diversion from his troubles.

With every step as he headed home, his weary body reminded him of his hard day's work. He tried not to think that his day was far from over. There were still snares to check and wood to gather.

Phillip took the shortcut through the woods that skirted town. Each time he bent to pick up a stick or a twig, his muscles ached and his bones throbbed. His blistered palms prickled. And with every puff of the gentle summer breeze, his sunburned cheeks and forearms stung.

The moment he entered the quiet house, Phillip headed straight for the hearth and went about the business of stoking the fire. His mother had set a pot of stew to gently simmering above it. Mutton, if his nose told him right. The turnips and spicy greens bubbling amid the meat caused his empty stomach to growl. He hadn't eaten a bite since breakfast.

Leah stepped up behind him and tapped his shoulder.

"You're dressed!" he observed, smiling. "Why, I hardly recognized you without that tattered old quilt tucked up under your chin."

She smiled sweetly. "It feels wonderful to be up and about again."

"I'm sure it does. But see you take care," he warned. "You could have a relapse."

Leah nodded. "That's what Mother says. But I'm feeling better than I have in weeks and weeks!" Her smile softened when she added, "And it's all thanks to you and White Wolf's—"

Phillip pressed a forefinger over his lips. "Shhh!" he warned. "If anyone learns that he gave me the cure, they're sure to think he's evil. And what they'd do to him if—"

"I'm sorry. Don't worry, I'll keep my promise." Then she brightened. "Did you know that Father was awake for awhile this afternoon?"

Phillip stood and tidied the wood piled beside the hearth. Many times during the day, he'd pictured his father's broken and battered body and prayed for a speedy recovery. "I'm glad to hear it."

"He wasn't awake long, but while he was, he told us that you saved his life."

Phillip took no comfort from Leah's words. *It was probably because he was so angry at me that he fell in the first place,* Phillip told himself for the hundredth time that day.

"Father said it all happened so fast. He didn't know how you had the presence of mind to grab that mattress and tuck it under him just in time." She clasped her hands in front of her. "He said he's very proud of the man you're becoming. He told Doc Turner that—"

"The doctor was here? Again?" Phillip's heart drummed with dread. Had the man told his father how he'd spoken to him? Had Mother?

Leah nodded. "He came back because he forgot his coat." She narrowed an eye and tilted her head. "Dr. Turner asked for you," she said. "Mother told him you were working at the feed and grain with Cousin George in Father's stead." Shrugging, she added, "He said he owed you an apology. He shouldn't have lost his temper with you."

He owes me an apology? Phillip was totally confused. *I wonder if even when I'm a man, I'll understand how people think.*

Chapter Twelve

Help for Leah

Leah insisted upon getting dressed every morning. Insisted, too, upon stashing her own bedroll. "I want to do my share," she'd explain, "so I'll feel like a real member of the family for a change!"

Twice now, she'd shouldered Phillip away from the basin, intent upon scrubbing pots and bowls. She did her level best to beat him to the back yard every morning to gather eggs and feed the chickens. She ignored Phillip and Mother's warnings that she might have a relapse.

No one could have guessed how quickly illness would set in. One minute, her mood was bright as a new-polished copper pot. The next, Leah's rosy cheeks and spirits had paled.

Nine days after Father's accident, Leah was forced to take to her bed again. Three days after that, Mother broke down under the strain.

For the next week, Phillip tried balancing his work at the shop with his work at home. He ran from the grain shed that was being built to the chickens that needed tending. He hammered at one place and cooked at the other.

It wasn't until he pulled a tape measure from his pocket to test Leah's fever that he realized he couldn't handle Father's and Mother's work as well as his own. Phillip decided he needed to ask for help.

With less than a month before the birth of her first child, Sarah had her hands full in her own home. But her husband, Jake, had been trained to care for the sick. He quickly agreed to help with the care of the three patients. John's wife, Hannah, volunteered to add a few extra potatoes to her pots of soup and stew. And John delivered the hearty meals to his parents' household.

With rest, Mother grew stronger. Things were running rather well under Phillip's direction!

He was hard at work on the final phase of the grain shed when Cousin George announced big news. "The freemen took a vote," George said, "and decided it's time we had both a schoolhouse *and* a place of worship. We've been hired to help build the new church!"

Phillip tried to show some enthusiasm at the news. Carpentry was honest work. It was a necessary profession worthy of respect. But Phillip had never wanted to be a carpenter.

As a very small boy, he thought he might like to be a mariner someday. A short trip across the bay proved his stomach wasn't suited to the ups and downs of the moody sea.

Later, Phillip decided a printer was what he wanted to be. But when Mr. Cooper told him he'd have to read every page three times—once to know what must be printed, once to set the type, and once to ensure a perfect copy—Phillip abandoned the idea. He did more than enough reading as a schoolboy!

And then Sarah brought home her future husband. Jake was a tall, burly young man with pitch black hair, eyes as blue as the sky, and a voice that reminded Phillip of thunder. Jake Donnelley vowed to his future father-in-law that with his training as an apothecary, he'd be able to provide well for Sarah.

Phillip wasn't impressed with Jake's size. Nor did the power of his voice influence him in the least. And why anyone in his right mind would want to marry his giggling older sister, he had no idea.

But Jake's eyes lit up when he spoke of the herbs and roots that soothed old people, suffering with rheumatism. His voice trembled with excitement when he discovered a better, quicker way to bring down a fever. His balms could cure a rash and stanch bleeding. Strong teas increased lagging heartbeats or eased the pain of childbirth.

As Phillip watched Jake, he realized that being an apothecary was special. Folks could build their own houses—perhaps not with the precision of a carpenter, but they could do it all the same. They could lay bricks. Dye wool. Spin cloth. Make watches. But in Phillip's mind, no one *helped* people the way those in Jake's profession did. Jake's work made a very real difference in people's everyday lives.

Phillip wanted *his* life's work to make a difference.

"Your pa is going to be right proud of the way you've taken to the craft, son." Cousin George's voice broke into Phillip's thoughts. "Imagine how the business will grow with all of us working together!"

Sighing, Phillip turned his attention to the fir door frame he was hammering into place. He'd planed and scribed the frame himself. George had taught him the difference between jack planes, long planes, smoothing planes, and rabbet planes. He'd learned to make ploughing planes and molding planes, round and hollow and snipe's bill planes.

After weeks of hard work, Phillip had learned to use every saw and hammer, every awl and gimlet almost as well a skilled carpenter. He could use them so well, in fact, that Cousin George promised to see that he got his very own set of tools as soon as possible.

"You're a natural!" George exclaimed no fewer than a dozen times every day. "Why, you're worth every bit of the sixpence I'm paying you!"

Phillip groaned to himself. His whole family seemed to expect him to become a carpenter. But Phillip would much rather spend eight years as an apprentice to an apothecary. He was more than willing to put in the hours and the work to achieve that title. If he ever became a partner to anyone, it would be to Jake.

But how could he break this news to his father?

Mother was waiting for Phillip at the edge of the woods when he left work for the day. "Phillip," she said. "I need your help."

He smiled, glad to see that she was feeling well enough to be out. "I'm happy to do anything for you, Mother."

She took his arm and said as they walked, "It's about Leah. I'm very worried about her."

Phillip nodded. "So am I. The quinsy really has a grip on her this time."

"She was doing so well while you were feeding her that . . .that brew." Stepping in front of him, Mother grasped his hands. "I want you to make up another batch right away."

"But Father said that I shouldn't—"

Mother stamped her tiny foot. "He never said anything of the kind! He wanted to know all the ingredients, so we'd be better informed in the event something in the tea made her sick."

Phillip frowned. "I don't know, Mother. It sounded to me as though Father didn't want me to—"

"He only asked what went into the cure," she repeated, squeezing his hands. "Never did he say we couldn't—"

"We?"

Mother looked toward the sky and shook her head. "Yes. I'll help you gather whatever you need—berries, roots, shoots—and I'll help you prepare it, too. I've already talked to Jake. He said you swore him to secrecy and that he wouldn't help me unless you gave your approval."

"But what will we do if Father—"

Mother raised her chin and rested both fists on her hips. "I'll talk to your father. You just get yourself over to Jake's shop and get busy making that tea!"

That said, she began to hurry toward their house, leaving a bewildered Phillip standing alone in the middle of the path. "Well," she said, "aren't you going?"

As Phillip started off toward Jake's shop, Mother called, "Make sure you get enough for your father, too."

When Phillip raised his brows and widened his eyes, she quickly added, "Well, it couldn't *hurt,* now could it?"

Phillip and Jake worked quickly to gather the ingredients for the tea.

"With Leah so ill," Jake said, "why don't you run home with this mixture now? Then you can come back here and we'll start on your next lessons before you go over to George's."

Not stopping to answer, Phillip grabbed the small pouch of precious herbs and ran as fast as he could toward home. Once there, he headed straight for the kitchen, where he quietly passed the pouch to Mother. "Tea," he whispered.

Mother hugged him fiercely. Her smiling eyes sent him a heartfelt 'thank you.' "Perhaps you'll stoke the fire for me and fill the kettle," she said, winking. "I'm in the mood to brew a nice hot cup of tea."

Understanding that the tea she'd brew would be for Leah, Phillip returned her grin. "Of course I will." He went right to work, poking the coals that glowed in the grate until the embers sparked flames that lapped the underside of the big iron pot. He added a chunk of wood to the top of the woodpile. Then he stepped onto the porch to dip the tea kettle into the rain barrel just outside the door. Adjusting the kettle's lid, he hung it by its handle on the big iron hook above the fire. While he waited for the water to boil, he swept up ashes from the hearth.

Soon Mother would spoon the powdered herbs into a mug of hot water and stir it well. She'd deliver it to Leah, who'd drink it down. In a few hours, Mother would begin the whole process again, and by this time tomorrow, they'd notice a marked improvement in Leah's condition. Phillip was so overjoyed he could have shouted his praises to the Lord above!

"Is that you, Phillip?" Father asked from his bed. "I want to discuss something with you before you head off to work. It's time we formally announced your apprenticeship."

"But Pastor Jenkins hired a new schoolteacher," Phillip protested. "I hear that he'll report for work in a few weeks and I can go back to school!"

Splints still held Father's arm and leg in place, but Dr. Turner had removed the bandages that had protected Father's cracked ribs.

"You already know how to read and write and cipher numbers," Father replied. "What you need to learn now is a craft so you can provide for yourself and your family someday. Any more schooling would be a waste of time."

Phillip remembered what Jake had said: *Study hard, and learn to read and write Latin. It isn't easy learning the sciences of medicine.* In order to step to the next phase of his education, his brother-in-law had told him, Phillip must first earn a certificate from—

"Phillip!" Father said. "I asked you a straight question, and I expect a straight answer."

"Sorry, Father," he said. "I guess I was daydreaming."

Father frowned. "You'd better bring your head down out of the clouds, son, before they completely fog your thoughts. Now tell me, how many more days will you be on the grain shed project?"

"Cousin George says we'll be able to wrap things up by the end of the week. Then we're to start right in on the new church."

Father nodded. "George tells me you must have been born with a hammer in your hand." Grinning slightly, he added, "He said you handle boards and tools well. Almost too well for a mere lad of twelve."

Phillip should have been honored by the compliment. Instead, his shoulders slumped as he wondered again how he would break the news to his father. He'd already promised Jake that the moment he was no longer needed to fill in for his father, he'd begin his apothecary apprenticeship.

Chapter Thirteen

The Freedom to Choose

A week later, Phillip was well into his secret training with Jake. He was amazed to learn that the work of an apothecary included more than preparing medicines. According to Jake, apothecaries also made preserves and sweets.

"The word itself, *apotheca*," Jake explained, "originally defined any kind of store or warehouse. The owner of such a place was called an *apothecarious*."

Mr. Jones, who had trained Jake, had himself learned the trade in England. He had served at courts and in the houses of great people. "Mr. Jones' favorite part of the job," Jake said, "was making sugared fruits. He was a grocer as much as an apothecary. He had to stock the ingredients for sweet treats."

Jake Donnelley was an Irish lad from County Mayo. He was the son of a servant and a gardener in one of those grand houses. An unlikely prospect for an apothecary's apprentice, Jake had bright eyes and a solid memory. Jones saw those traits in Jake and decided that he'd take the boy on.

"I decided early on," Jake added, "that I wanted no part of the grocer end of the business."

He looked around to make sure no one else was listening. Then he whispered to Phillip, "Whenever any of the old fashioned folks asked me to whip up a batch of sweets, I deliberately under-sugared everything." Laughing, he added, "I earned a reputation for being a skilled druggist and a terrible cook!"

"I'm glad we're concentrating on the medical side of the business," Phillip admitted. "I did enough cooking while Mother and Leah had the measles to last me a lifetime!"

"In England," Jake told Phillip, "in a hall near Bridge Street are two magnificent laboratories that supply all the surgeons' chests with medicine. They also supply the entire British Navy."

The profession, Phillip quickly learned, was populated by

men familiar with the practice and theory of chemistry. "Without an extensive education, we can't hope to prepare wholesome, helpful remedies," Jake said.

As they worked, Phillip and Jake discussed the many lives saved by serious-minded apothecaries. They also talked about the lives that were lost when the druggist allowed himself to lose sight of even the smallest detail.

"There's talk in England of passing an Act of Parliament that would forbid apothecaries from serving as constables, or ward and parish offices, or as jurors."

"But why?" Phillip wanted to know.

"Some people are afraid we have the power to drug folks, and would use that knowledge to get them to do things our way."

Phillip shrugged. "Sounds like something our leaders in Boston could use. Then so many folks wouldn't be leaving to join Roger Williams."

Jake laughed heartily and dropped a good-natured thump on Phillip's back. "You're wise beyond your years, Phillip, but I think that's an opinion you'd be smart to keep to yourself! Now step out back and hoe the weeds in the garden."

If Mother had told Phillip to do the same chore, he would have complained to himself that it was woman's work. But Jake had made the importance of a well-tended garden very clear. The trees, plants, shrubs, and grasses that grew behind the apothecary shop were the backbone of his business. Besides, Jake's salary was more than fair at eighty pounds a year.

As he knelt between the plant rows, Phillip tested his

memory: “Yarrow is an insect repellent, and its leaves are useful in curing intestinal problems. Cornflowers are an astringent and a stimulant. They also increase urine flow. Ragwort cleanses the bowels.”

It was difficult growing species out of season. Doing so demanded special care. “Woody horsetail,” Phillip continued as he plucked weeds from between the plants. “This plant is used for ailments of the heart and can also be used to relieve congested lungs and epidemic dropsy.”

The hollyhock was by far Phillip’s favorite plant. Its roots, leaves, flowers, and seeds could all be put to use. “Hydrangea bark can be chewed to quiet a troubled stomach, mashed into a poultice for sore muscles, or brewed into a tea to stop vomiting. The root of the dwarf iris, smashed up and mixed with suet and beeswax, makes a good salve for sores.”

Phillip stared for a moment at the bright yellow blossoms of the Black-eyed Susan, trying to remember its many medicinal properties. After a moment, it came to him. “The liquids taken from the roots can be brewed into a healing lotion to relieve sores and snakebites, or a drink that can remedy dropsy, or drops that will relieve earaches.”

The lady slipper, like the hollyhock and the Black-eyed Susan, had many uses. “Potions made from this plant can relieve muscle spasms, fits, hysteria, and pain and can ward off the symptoms of stomach distress or relieve the sniffles.”

Pleased with his work—and his memorized lessons—Phillip left the garden to see what else Jake might have for him to do.

"Cousin George and John still need you to work on the new church," Jake reminded him. "I promised them I wouldn't keep you too long or tire you out too badly to be of use to them," he said, laughing. "Now be on your way, m'boy, before George sends a search party out looking for you."

"You won't tell them I was studying—"

Jake gently chucked Phillip under the chin. "I gave my word, didn't I? You'll make the announcement when you're ready. 'Til then, the lessons are between us."

Phillip glanced at the jars and bottles, crocks and pots that lined the shelves of Jake's shop. Did any of them contain a mixture that would give him the courage to tell Father that his youngest son would not be following in his footsteps?

George gave Phillip the task of delivering boards and planks to the place where they'd build the new church. Back and forth he drove the wagon. It seemed to take forever before all the materials for the job had been delivered to the building site.

When he finished, Phillip guided the wagon into the shed out back. He unharnessed Sweet Bessie, George's grey speckled mare, and led her into the barn at the back of the property. He put the same energy and determination into brushing the old horse that he'd put into learning to hammer and saw. Soon, her coat glowed with a healthy sheen that reminded Phillip of the wet granite rocks near the banks of Mystic River.

Phillip used the time to study his apothecary lessons. He

practiced Jake's lists every chance he got. All the way home, he recited the healing properties of special medicines. Each time his right foot hit the ground, he named a plant. When the left foot touched down, he listed its healing properties.

"Muskrat root. . .sore throat. Wild rhubarb. . .cleanses the bowels. Sumac root. . .toothaches. Juniper. . .increase urine flow. Wild geranium. . .astringent. Indian turnip. . .relief from stomach gas."

Once he got home, Phillip continued to practice his apothecary list but he was careful to recite his lessons silently: *Stinkweed. Sage. Fern. Bear grass.*

"Phillip." Father's stern voice broke Phillip's deep concentration, making him start with fright. "Tell me where you were this morning?"

"Why, I was with John and Cousin George at the workshop, of course." It wasn't the *whole* truth, but it *was* the truth.

"George stopped by here at daybreak to save you the walk into town, but you'd already left."

Phillip's heart pounded and his palms grew damp.

"Where were you, if not at the grain shed?"

Could he confess that he'd been studying at the apothecary shop with Jake? *Should* he tell the truth and risk putting his brother-in-law on his father's bad side, too? Was there a way to tell Father that he had no desire to become an apprentice carpenter?

"Don't tell me you're off in dreamland again." Father's arm no longer required the splint or the sling, and he crossed both arms over his chest. "Where were you, if not at the grain shed?" he repeated, his voice louder than before.

"George asked that I bring the lumber for the church to the building site."

"You know very well that I'm not talking about what you did this afternoon. I want to know where you went when you left home this morning."

Mother came into the parlor, biting her lower lip and wringing her hands. "William, I wonder if you've seen my sewing kit. It seems I've misplaced it. I have socks to darn and—"

Father blinked. It wasn't like Mother to interrupt him. "Abigail," he began, his voice gentling slightly. "I have no idea where your sewing basket is." He sighed, then leaned back in his high-backed wooden rocker. "Have you looked in the kitchen cupboard?"

"I have," she said, nodding and smiling. "It's as though the silly thing grew legs and walked off! It was there yesterday, when I mended the pocket in your breeches."

"Where did you sit to do this mending?"

"Why, in the chair beside the hearth, as always."

"Then I should think you'll find your missing sewing kit there, on the hearth." He sent her a tired smile. "Why don't you see if it's not there?"

Mother focused on her husband's face once more and gave a little nod. "Thank you, William. Whatever would I do without you!"

Father waited until she was out of earshot before he said, "I dare say, all the stress and strain of these last few months is still taking its toll on your mother. We'll have to take care to protect her from any further distress."

"You're right, Father."

Father aimed his dark brown gaze straight into Phillip's eyes. "Now, back to the subject at hand," he said.

A small sweet voice called out from the other room. "I found it dear."

"That's nice, Abigail." Father zeroed in on Phillip again. "Now—"

"Right where you said it would be!" Mother added.

Father took a deep breath. "Abigail, I know what you're up to, and it isn't working."

Silence from the kitchen told Phillip they would not be interrupted again.

"Now, then," Father continued. "You were about to tell me where you went when you left here this morning."

Phillip took a deep breath. *Please, Lord,* he prayed, *give me the strength to say what I must, and the wisdom to say it well.*

"I went to Jake's shop."

Father's brows drew together in a confused frown. "To Jake's shop? But whatever for?"

"I was helping Jake."

Father chuckled. "Don't you have enough to do? You're doing your chores and Leah's and helping your mother and filling in for me at the workshop. Now you're working for Jake, too?"

Phillip nodded.

That nod said far more than he'd intended.

"You're interested in Jake's work, then?"

"I am, Father."

"I'll give you this much. It's a fascinating profession." Father cocked one brow. "But what's the point of hanging around Jake, even for a morning, when your future is already planned for you?"

"I'll likely be spending a good deal of time in Jake's shop," he began. "But you can be sure I'll only go when I've seen to my other duties," he quickly added.

"He's a good man, I'll grant you. But what you need to secure your future as a carpenter is time on the job, not time in Jake's shop."

"My future *isn't* as a carpenter. I want to be an apothecary. Jake has agreed to let me apprentice with him. It'll take eight years, and he says I'll have to work hard and study long to earn the title. But I'm no shirker, Father."

Phillip didn't give Father a chance to say anything. "I'll put in the time and effort required. I'll put the lessons you've taught me into practice, too. Like, never do a thing halfway. Or if you can't do your level best, don't do the thing at all. I'll be the best apothecary you've ever seen. I'll make you and Mother proud. You'll see!"

How he got it all out, Phillip didn't know. Perhaps the little prayer he'd said helped more than he thought it would!

Somehow, Father got to his feet. He leaned on the two crutches he'd whittled from scraps of oak. "My father was a woodworker, and his father before him. It's an honorable profession. Your own brother was proud to accept it."

Father thumped the floor with one crutch. "Why, Jesus Himself was a carpenter. The work wasn't too good for Him. Yet *you're* above it!"

Phillip shook his head. "No, Father. I never said I didn't respect you *or* your chosen profession. You're right. It's an honorable trade—one any man would be proud to claim as his own."

"I don't understand," Father said. "Help me understand, son."

Phillip stared at the toes of his boots. When he met Father's eyes, tears were stinging in his own. "It's an honorable trade, one any man would be proud to claim as his own," he repeated, "if it's his choice. If it's what he wants to do."

"Wants? Wants!" Father fell back into the rocker. "Who led you to believe life offers you *choices,* boy? Have you been off in the woods reading Leah's fairy tales? I didn't *choose* carpentry. Carpentry chose *me*. It's what Smythes *do*. That's all there is to it."

"It's what Smythes *have done*," Phillip said. "You braved the long, dangerous voyage across the Atlantic on board the *Mayflower.* You risked everything you had to come to the New World. Why did you do it, Father, if not to claim the freedom to choose?"

For a long moment, Father did not speak. Finally, he said, "Go to Jake, then, since it's his life you choose. But see that you earn your keep and take pride in your behavior, for you can't choose a new name."

"But Father—"

Father held up a hand. "Here's the thing about choices, Phillip," he said. "Once made, a man must learn to live with them." There were tears in his eyes when he looked up to his son. "I pray you'll be able to live with yours."

CHAPTER FOURTEEN

The Capture of White Wolf

Phillip lay in bed, fuming. He couldn't believe how Father reacted to his announcement about wanting to be an apothecary. The more he thought about it, the angrier he became.

"I'm not staying here one more minute," he whispered into his pillow. "I'll do my morning chores because Mother and

Leah need my help, but I'm not sleeping under this roof."

Silently, Phillip slipped out of bed. He quietly gathered a few things in his bedroll and dropped them, along with his shoes, out the window. It was quiet downstairs. Were Mother and Father sound asleep?

Phillip kneeled by the loft ladder and strained his ears. The only sound he could hear was the gentle breathing of his parents and sister. His feet dressed only in socks, Phillip took one cautious step down the ladder. Silence. Rung by rung, he crept down to the main floor.

Suddenly he froze. The sounds of sheets and blankets rustling filled his ears. Had someone woken up? Phillip held his breath for what seemed like hours. The sound of breathing continued, someone had only rolled over in bed. Letting his breath out slowly, he tiptoed through the kitchen to the back door, remembering just in time to avoid the squeaky floorboard by the fire.

Once outside, Phillip crept around the corner of the house to gather his bedroll. Then he grabbed a rusting lantern from the porch. Following the moonlit path, he snuck out of town to the one place he knew would be safe: The cave.

Weeks before, White Wolf had returned to his people. Phillip could still remember his joy when he'd learned his friend had decided to follow Jesus Christ instead of the gods of his people. No trace of White Wolf's presence in the cave could be found. Phillip vowed that when his own visit to the cave ended, he'd show the same care.

Sleep didn't come that first dark, lonely night. Phillip turned the scene with his father over and over in his mind. Could he have announced his decision more gently? Should he have told his father of his decision at a different time and place?

Before the sun rose that next morning, Phillip retraced his route back to home. Avoiding his father, he quickly did his chores and headed for town, intent on carrying out his work. When he showed up at the new job site, John and Cousin George were already hard at work, digging the church's foundation.

"Didn't expect to see you here today," John admitted.

"Why not? I gave my word I'd work in Father's stead, didn't I?"

Chuckling, George said, "Your pa has already been here and gone. He told us the whole sorry story."

Phillip stood tall. So they knew what a disappointment he was to his father. *Never mind that,* Phillip told himself. *You have work to do, so do it.* "Where do you need me today, Cousin George?"

The man grinned and narrowed one eye. "You're a spunky boy, I'll give you that." Then, with a short laugh, he pointed toward the stack of lumber behind him. "We'll need fourteen planks, ten feet long each. And when you've got those cut, we'll need fourteen more that are eight feet long."

Phillip headed straight for the lumber pile, grabbing a rule and saw on the way. Fashioning a work table by placing board scraps between two tree stumps, he laid the planks down, one at a time. He measured the boards twice and squared each carefully before cutting.

When he was done, he asked for more work. George told him to scribe trim moldings from lengths of silver maple. The task required attention to detail and a steady hand. Phillip focused on the wood, so that when the frames were hung around the doors and windows of the church, Bostonians would say, "Phillip Smythe is responsible for those!" and his father would be proud.

When his long day ended, Phillip went home. In silence, he did his chores and ate his dinner. Saying he was tired and wanted to go to bed early, he once again snuck out to the cave.

White Wolf greeted Phillip. "You come to the cave to seek answers to prayers?"

"White Wolf!" he said. "I thought you were gone for good."

The Narragansett shook his head. "I sensed that my friend was unhappy. I have come to listen. Sit," he directed. "Tell me what makes your heart heavy."

Phillip sat on the floor and shared his story with White Wolf. The Indian got out some dried venison for them to snack on. They dipped a pottery bowl from White Wolf's beaded backpack into the stream that ran through the cave. The water tasted refreshing.

As they finished their snack, Phillip sighed. He didn't know which had exhausted him more—his hard day's work or telling his story.

"White Wolf has a son, too," the Narragansett said. "I

understand what beats in your father's heart. If he loves his child as I love mine, he would die in his son's place."

Phillip shrugged. "I prayed long and hard before making my decision," he admitted to White Wolf. "I believe in my heart that God wants me to be a healer, that He wants me to use His gifts to help people."

The Indian only nodded. After a time, he said, "The Great Spirit is wise and knows all things. I, too, have prayed for your future." The Indian paused. "God will guide you because you are wise enough to ask for guidance."

The lonely boy gave the Indian a long look. "You are my friend, aren't you?"

Smiling, White Wolf said, "I am proud to call you 'friend.' "

The next morning, White Wolf told Phillip to get Jake and return to the cave. To Phillip's surprise, when he and Jake arrived, White Wolf had been joined by Black Eagle, the Narragansett healer. The four sat together in a circle and Jake and Black Eagle began talking about healing medicine. The old man listened intently to everything Phillip's brother-in-law said. Jake, in turn, gave his full attention to the wise old Indian

At the end of the meeting, Jake hurried home to write Black Eagle's ingredients in his apothecary book. Black Eagle admitted that he would add Jake's suggestions to the remedies of his people.

Words were not necessary when White Wolf and Phillip met in the cave that evening. Together, they'd witnessed a miracle.

In the morning, White Wolf would return to his people.

"I will miss you," Phillip admitted.

"And I, you. But we will see one another again. The Spirit assures me of this."

Phillip fell asleep, grateful for the friendship of this good man. Grateful, too, for the secrets he'd shared. Phillip knew that without them, Leah would probably have died.

The thundering of a dozen horses' hooves and the bellowing of many angry men woke Phillip and his friend. Torch light blazed into the cave.

"*There's* the savage!" Mr. Grover, the town's cooper, spoke first.

Mr. Harold, Boston's brazier, said, "You're coming with us, heathen!"

A man Phillip didn't recognize added, "You are evil."

"And you'll pay for your heathen ways with your life!" said the saddler, Joshua Edwards.

In one heartbeat, they'd surrounded White Wolf. In the next, they'd tied and gagged him.

"Stop!" Phillip insisted. "You're making a mistake. He's no savage. This is my friend, White Wolf. He is a member of the Narragansett tribe and—"

"Quiet, boy!" Mr. Grover barked. "We don't care what kind of savage he is. His skin is red."

"Made all the redder by the fires of hell!" a man in the back interrupted.

"Proof enough he's a demon in disguise!"

"But he's done nothing," Phillip insisted, standing at White Wolf's side.

"It was his *potion* that you fed your sister," Edwards snarled.

"And it cured her!" Phillip pointed out.

Mr. Harold's eyes were slits when he grated out, "Evil disguises itself in many ways. The only way to protect our women and children is to kill him. To kill *all* Indians. They're pagan savages, one and all, sent by Satan to slaughter and destroy us."

"He's not a pagan!" Phillip shrieked as they slung his friend over the back of an unsaddled horse. "He's a Christian! Why, he learned English from a missionary. He reads and writes it, too! He prays to God for guidance."

"Heathen!" someone shouted, as though Phillip hadn't said a word.

"Savage!" another voice yelled.

Mr. Grover grabbed Phillip's arm. "Don't interfere with us, boy, if you know what's good for you. We're God-fearing men, and we'll abide by God's law." He looked at his men and winked wickedly. "He'll get a fair trial—"

"Before we burn him for his sin!" Mr. Edwards interrupted, laughing.

"But what is his sin?" Phillip demanded, stepping in front of White Wolf. "Being born a Narragansett?"

Mr. Grover's hold on his arm tightened. "Now you're seeing the light!" He waved another raider over. "Tie the boy up good and tight; it'll keep him out of our way while we're about the Lord's business."

Phillip wriggled free of the man's grasp. He darted between the stomping, whinnying horses and ran full speed toward the mouth of the cave. "Don't worry, White Wolf. I'll stop them. I'll stop them if it kills me!" he shouted as he disappeared into the woods.

From his hiding place in the low-growing shrubs, Phillip listened to the loud laughter of the crowd echoing menacingly from deep within the cave. "Let's head back to town," he heard Mr. Grover command. "The sooner we start, the sooner we can finish God's work!"

When the dust of the pounding horses' hooves settled, Phillip ran for all he was worth. *Lord, God,* he prayed, *keep White Wolf safe 'til I can round up some help!*

Somehow, the men had learned that White Wolf had taught Phillip the healing secrets of his people. It didn't matter to them that those secrets had saved Leah's life.

Phillip had promised to choose wisely and carefully when sharing the Indians' secrets. Leah and Jake knew, of course. And his parents and John and Sarah might suspect that the herb brew came from an Indian. Surely every one of them could be trusted.

Phillip had no way of knowing *how* the men had learned about the healer's brew. He only knew that White Wolf should not pay with his life for sharing Black Eagle's life-saving secret with his white friends!

He had to find a way to save White Wolf. If he couldn't, he'd live with the man's gruesome death on his conscience all the days of his life.

The same torches that would light the deadly fire now provided the beacon that guided Phillip as he ran blindly through the night, eyes stinging in the trailing cloud of their horses' dust. When at last he reached the town square, breathless and exhausted, his heart hammered with dread at the sight.

White Wolf stood lashed to the stake!

Phillip realized the awful truth. These men had been plotting White Wolf's death for some time. They hadn't been back in town long enough to gather the wood for a fire. They must have stacked the wood around the center post long before heading out in search of White Wolf.

They've been watching me, Phillip realized. *I led them straight to White Wolf!*

Fury boiled within him at the sight of the curious onlookers who had gathered to witness the grisly event. He must do something to stop it.

Phillip raced forward, forcing his way between the pack of men until he stood at the front of the crowd. There, at the edge of the circle of logs and twigs around White Wolf's feet, stood Jackson Grover, leader of the crowd. He held his burning torch high. Every eye watched him.

"This man," he said in a deep, ominous voice, "will die

tonight because of his unrepentance. The many gods he has worshiped will not save him from his fate! 'And he shall say, Where are their gods, their rock in whom they trusted?' " Mr. Grover said, quoting Deuteronomy 32:37.

He held up his hands, commanding silence from the chanting, unruly crowd. When they had quieted, he quoted Jeremiah 5:19. " 'As you have forsaken me, and served strange gods in your land, so shall ye serve strangers in a land that is not yours!' "

Mr. Grover leaned close and spat in White Wolf's face, "Your new home will be in *hell*!"

It was a maddening, frightening scene. Phillip's mind raced. White Wolf was a man of selfless deeds who loved God. Why, then, didn't these men see in White Wolf what *he'd* seen?

"Judge not that ye be not judged," they proclaimed in their prayers. But they were willing to judge White Wolf's deeds based on nothing more than his appearance.

Phillip had to find a way to open their eyes to the truth.

"Kill him!" the men in the crowd shouted, shaking their fists at the Indian. "Burn him 'til he breathes no more!"

Phillip could see the murderous light in their wild eyes. He could stand no more. Jumping onto the pile of sticks and twigs, he faced the crowd. " 'He that is without sin among you, let him first cast a stone,' " Phillip recited.

Mr. Grover, stood with feet wide apart and shook his flaming torch at the crowd. "Listen to that!" he told them, laughing, "The boy's quoting the Good Book!"

Phillip knew that every moment White Wolf's chances for safety were growing smaller. He ripped the flaming torch out of Mr. Grover's grasp. " 'He that is without sin among you, let him first cast a stone,' " Phillip repeated.

The shouts of the crowd lowered to a low drone.

"The boy's gone daft," someone said.

"He's taken leave of his senses!" said another voice as Mr. Grover struggled to regain hold of the torch. "Turn it loose," the man yelled. "Can't you see the sparks are falling on the kindling! *You'll* set the fire. I thought you said 'let he who is without sin cast the first—' "

Phillip got both hands on the torch handle. With a mighty tug, he wrestled it away from Mr. Grover. "I *am* a sinner!" he shouted as he stamped out the sparks that fell into the dried weeds and grasses beneath the woodpile. "I never pretended *not* to be!"

A hush fell over the men who had gathered round. For a moment, they merely looked at each other.

"Are you going to just stand there like a bunch of old women and let this slip of a lad keep you from doing God's work!" Mr. Grover bellowed.

The crowd stood frowning. The men looked from the Indian to the boy to Mr. Grover.

"Well, *are* you?"

"We are *not!*" Mr. Edwards said, stepping forward. "Either you're with us or you're against us," he challenged, facing the quiet men. "What's it going to be?"

CHAPTER FIFTEEN

Free to Dream

"No!" Phillip yelled as the angry men advanced. "Don't do it! If you kill White Wolf, you will have to answer to God for what you've—"

"What is going on here!"

The men, Phillip, even White Wolf turned to face the man who stood on the fringes of the crowd, demanding an explanation for the commotion.

"William," Mr. Grover began, "it's good to see you're up and about at last. We have serious work to do here. Stand aside, man, and let us do what must be done."

Father hobbled closer, leaning on his crutch and on his small, trembling daughter. "I'll *not* stand aside and watch you commit cold-blooded murder."

A crazy grin covered Mr. Grover's face. "Hardly cold-blooded," he laughed, "since we plan to boil his blood!"

No one shared in the man's sick joke. He frowned and tried a new approach. " 'Thou shalt give life for life, eye for eye, tooth for tooth.' "

Father interrupted. " 'Ye have heard that it hath been said, an eye for an eye, and a tooth for a tooth: But I say unto you, That ye resist not evil: but whosoever shall smite thee on thy right cheek, turn to him the other also.' "

He paused as the crowd quieted down. " 'Be ye therefore perfect, even as your Father which is in heaven is perfect.' "

Father faced the crowd. He pointed with his crutch at Mr. Edwards, at Mr. Grover, at Mr. Harold. "Christ Jesus was born and died on the cross so the wicked would not twist His Father's words as you're doing now. This man has done no wrong."

"But, he fed your sweet Leah the Devil's drink!" Mr. Grover insisted.

Father laughed harshly. He looked down at Leah's trusting face. "Does she look evil to you?" He repeated the question to the crowd. "Well, does she?"

The men stood silently, thinking about Father's question. It was as they pondered what he'd said that Phillip's father nodded toward his son. "Hand me that torch, Phillip."

The boy did not move.

"Phillip, I asked you to hand over the torch."

"I can't, Father."

Father stepped forward, supported by the crutch on his left and Leah on his right. "Yes, son, you can," he said gently, releasing Leah to extend his hand.

"It's okay, Phillip," Leah whispered. "You can trust Father."

When Phillip still made no move to give him the torch, Father closed his eyes and hung his head. When he lifted his head again, he focused on the crowd.

"I have wronged my son, just as you have wronged this Indian."

He met Phillip's eyes, then faced the crowd again and continued. "The rules I imposed on my son were not decreed by God. They were, instead, set down by my own hand."

Father's speech was a public apology. Phillip couldn't believe that his father was admitting a weakness in front of every man in town. He handed Father the torch.

"You are a fine boy, Phillip," Father said. "One day soon, you'll be a fine man—free to seek your dreams."

You'll be a fine man, his father had said. White Wolf had told him, *I'm proud to call you 'friend.'* If God had chosen that moment to call Phillip home to heaven, he would have left this world happy and fulfilled!

He walked with calm deliberation to where the men had tied the Indian to the stake, removed the dirty rag they'd stuffed into his mouth, and began loosening the tight ropes that bound his wrists and ankles.

"William Smythe has never led a man astray," said a voice from the back of the crowd. "He's a good and decent man who keeps his opinions to himself and does his work well. What more can be asked of a man? If he says let the Indian go, we should give it some thought!"

Phillip, with White Wolf at his side, answered: " 'The law of the Lord is perfect, converting the soul: the testimony of the Lord is sure, making wise the simple.' "

"He speaks the truth," Pastor Jenkins cried, hurrying up the street from his house where the noise had awakened him. He held out his hand to Leah, who smiled sweetly and took it.

"But. . .but he's an Indian!" Mr. Grover stammered. "The Pequots slaughtered whole families as they traveled from Boston to Salem. Narragansett, Pequot, what difference does it make what tribe they belong to. Red men are all alike. You know it's true! We must take our revenge. It will show them they cannot get away with—"

The preacher pointed a finger at Mr. Grover. "Remember what the Good Book says," he thundered. " 'Vengeance is mine, sayeth the Lord.' " Then, facing the crowd once more, Pastor Jenkins added, "All of you, go home and sit with your wives and children. Beg the Lord's forgiveness for what you were about to do here tonight."

Slowly, the crowd thinned. Men shuffled quietly away from the town square, heads hung in shame.

White Wolf grasped Phillip's shoulder. "I was wise to call you friend, for tonight, you saved my life."

"As you saved my daughter's when you shared the secrets of your healer's brew," Father added. "You are welcome to sup with us this night."

Leah shyly approached the tall man. "Thank you, sir, for telling Phillip how to make me better. I will never forget you. Won't you please eat with us before you go?"

White Wolf smiled at Leah. "I am proud to have helped you. But I cannot stay. I must return to my people."

William nodded. "Then will you join us on your next visit to Boston?"

"I will."

Phillip, Father, and Leah watched as the proud Narragansett walked toward the woods. When he disappeared from view, Phillip tossed Father's crutch aside.

"Lean on me, Father," he said, slipping Father's arm around his shoulders.

"And on me," Leah added, mimicking her older brother's gesture.

Father and son locked gazes as they headed for the Smythe house.

"I am proud to call you 'son,' " William said.

"And I am proud to call you 'Father.' "

There was no need to say more.

Good News for Readers

There's more!

Phillip and Leah's adventures continue in *Fire by Night.* Phillip is caught in Boston Harbor during a huge cyclone that flattens much of Boston. Then Father must leave for England to build furniture for the King and earn much-needed money. Having just gotten used to Father's absence the Smythe family is awakened by a fire in the night. Their home burns to the ground, and the fire has been set by John's enemies.

When will Father return? Will John ever become more like the man everyone knew? And how can Phillip and Leah help their family recover from the destruction of the fire that ravaged their home?

Further Reading

Avi, James Watling. *Finding Providence: The Story of Roger Williams.* New York: HarperCollins, 1997.

Dexter, Lincoln. *Maps of Early Massachusetts*. Sturbridge, Mass.: Lincoln Dexter, 1984.

Duey, Kathleen. Sarah Anne Hartford: Massachusetts, 1651. American Diaries, no. 1. New York: Aladdin, 1996.

Fleischmann, Paul. Saturnalia. New York: HarperCollins, 1992.

Simmons, William S. and Frank W. Porter. *The Narragansett.* Philadelphia: Chelsea House, 1989.

Speare, Elizabeth George. *The Witch of Blackbird Pond.* Boston: Houghton Mifflin, 1958.

Terkel, Susan Neiburg. *Colonial American Medicine*. New York: Franklin Watts, 1993.

Index